Twel
Twelve i
One UNIFO

Don't miss a
12-book continuity series, featuring irresistible
soldiers from all branches of the armed forces.

Now serving—
those reckless and wild flyboys in the U.S. Air Force...

TAILSPIN
by Cara Summers
July 2011

HOT SHOT
by Jo Leigh
August 2011

NIGHT MANEUVERS
by Jillian Burns
September 2011

Uniformly Hot!—
The Few. The Proud. The Sexy as Hell!

Blaze

Dear Reader,

One of the last movies River Phoenix ever made was called *Dogfight*. It was about a young marine about to ship off to Vietnam in 1963. He and his buddies throw a party the night before called a Dogfight. The guy who brings the ugliest girl wins. So River finds a plain girl and asks her to the party. At the last minute, he tries to back out, but it's too late. Of course, she finds out what the party is really about, and he spends the rest of the night trying to make it up to her and ultimately falling for her.

River's character is a deeply flawed young man, hardened by a brutal childhood, yet eventually redeemed by love. Ahh, my favorite kind of hero. My hero Mitch McCabe is a flawed, bitter guy, too. And I knew I'd need just the right heroine to make him believe in love. When Alex appeared in *Let It Ride,* I knew she was the right one for Mitch. Who better for him to trust implicitly than his best buddy?

Enjoy,

Jillian Burns

Jillian Burns

NIGHT MANEUVERS

™ **Harlequin**®

TORONTO NEW YORK LONDON
AMSTERDAM PARIS SYDNEY HAMBURG
STOCKHOLM ATHENS TOKYO MILAN MADRID
PRAGUE WARSAW BUDAPEST AUCKLAND

Recycling programs
for this product may
not exist in your area.

ISBN-13: 978-0-373-79638-0

NIGHT MANEUVERS

ABOUT THE AUTHOR

Jillian Burns has always read romance, and spent her teens immersed in the worlds of Jane Eyre and Elizabeth Bennett. She lives in Texas with her husband of twenty years and their three active kids. Jillian likes to think her emotional nature—sometimes referred to as *moodiness*—has found the perfect outlet in writing stories filled with passion and romance. She believes romance novels have the power to change lives with their message of eternal love and hope.

Books by Jillian Burns

HARLEQUIN BLAZE

466—LET IT RIDE
572—SEDUCE AND RESCUE
602—PRIMAL CALLING

To get the inside scoop on Harlequin Blaze and its talented writers, be sure to check out blazeauthors.com.

Don't miss any of our special offers. Write to us at the following address for information on our newest releases.

Harlequin Reader Service
U.S.: 3010 Walden Ave., P.O. Box 1325, Buffalo, NY 14269
Canadian: P.O. Box 609, Fort Erie, Ont. L2A 5X3

To Tommy
for putting up with my deadline crunch times.
To Pam and Linda—
as always, couldn't do it without you.
And to Elizabeth,
for breaking the tie.
To Jennifer for great insights,
and to Barb for encouragement and support.
It really does take a village to raise a book.
And, as always, to my amazing editor Kathryn
for trusting that this story could be something,
despite everything, and making it so.

This book is dedicated to
all the children of alcoholics.

1

IF SHE EVER got married in a place like this, her mother would weep and wail for a month of Sundays.

Captain Alexandria Hughes, unlikely bridesmaid, looked around the small Las Vegas chapel, taking in the garish pink and purple drapery swags and the fake marble pedestals holding bouquets of fake white roses. The dozens of white candles weren't too bad, but…the Elvis impersonator in the cheap gold jacket would have to go.

Or maybe not. Maybe her mother would be so grateful if Alex ever married at all that Mom would even agree to let Elvis officiate.

The lone daughter in a family of three sons, Alex had been her mother's only hope for all things girly. Unfortunately, Alex had always preferred roping calves to baking pies. But that had never stopped Mom from trying. Even after twelve years, she still hoped Alex's

Air Force career was merely a rebellious phase that would end when she met Mr. Right.

The wedding march suddenly blared from speakers. She let all thoughts of Mom slip to the back of her mind and turned with the dozen or so guests to watch the bride walk down the aisle.

God, Jordan looked beautiful in that strapless white dress. The material shimmered and the full skirt flowed down to the pink shag carpet and swished when she walked.

Alex flattened her palm and pushed at an ache in her stomach. Must be nerves for her friend. She could never rock a wedding dress like that. For one thing, she had nothing in front to hold it up. For another, she'd have tripped over all that material puddling around her feet.

Luckily, she'd obtained permission to wear her dress uniform even though the wedding wasn't being held on base. She preferred her uniform to one of those froufrou dresses. Her uniform was familiar, comfortable. The only primping she'd done was shining her dress shoes and polishing her saber. The amount of fuss most women put into their looks had always seemed so ridiculous.

Until recently.

Major Cole Jackson, er…former Major Jackson of the U.S. Air Force—now *Officer* Jackson of the Las Vegas Police Department—beamed at his bride as she advanced down the aisle. Pure love for Jordan shone in his eyes and Alex felt a stab of…was that envy?

Nah. Jackson was a good buddy. After what he'd been through in Iraq, he deserved happiness. She'd about busted a gut cheering for them when he and Jordan had announced their engagement.

It was just the look that came over Jackson whenever he gazed at his fiancée. Like she was the missing part of his soul. Even the toughest airman might get a little knot in his throat watching that. Even McCabe.

Alex glanced over at Captain Mitchell McCabe, aka the best man. Okay, so maybe not McCabe. He was too busy winking at the redheaded maid of honor standing in front of Alex.

She clenched her teeth. What a player. But she cleared her expression and smiled as Jordan stepped up and took her groom's hand.

The vows were short and sweet, even with Elvis curling his lip and swinging his hips to punctuate each statement. Pastor Elvis pronounced Jackson and Jordan husband and wife and then Alex and five of her fellow uniformed officers pivoted to face each other, drew their sabers, and formed the arch.

Jackson—looking fit and strong in a simple black tuxedo—extended his elbow to his bride. They passed beneath the arch and kissed. After Lieutenant Colonel Grady issued the command to return sabers to belts, everyone headed into the next room for cake and champagne.

Whew. It was over. Maybe now Alex could get something to drink and go prop up a wall somewhere. She removed her white gloves and spent the next twenty minutes nursing her beer and glaring at McCabe's seduction routine as he hit on the redhead.

Never mind his practiced words. All Mitch had to do was stand there and women flocked to him. Even with the short military cut, his blond hair begged for a woman's fingers to run through it. His mischievous light blue eyes and tall, muscular build were simply icing on the cake. And when he smiled? Forget it, women were down for the count. Those twin dimples were the strongest weapon in his arsenal, and even his slightly crooked teeth only added charm to his deadly grin.

Fury ramped up as Alex watched him. When she'd returned to Nellis Air Force base after a two-year stint at Langley, she'd hoped to find he'd gotten past his I've-been-screwed-by-my-ex-wife-and-now-I'm-just-here-for-the-party phase. But it'd been seven years since his divorce, and, if anything, McCabe was worse now. She'd thought losing that bet with Jackson, forcing him to be celibate, might be the beginning of change for Mitch. But he'd seemed to make it through the ordeal unscathed.

"Alex, come get in the picture." Jordan took her elbow and led her to stand in front of the table where the cake and punch had been served.

The photographer fiddled with the tripod.

McCabe lined up next to Alex as Jordan gathered more people into the picture. "Aren't you going to find someone to go home with, Hughes?" McCabe murmured into her ear. After a dozen years of friendship, it irritated her how his Southern drawl still flowed through her core like premium oil through an engine. "It's practically required at weddings, isn't it?" He winked at the redhead.

"I think you've made the quota for both of us." She swiped her hat out from beneath her arm and clasped it behind her back.

"Aw, Hughes." McCabe grimaced. "What happened to you at Langley? Two years away from Nellis and you're no fun anymore." He scooted closer and placed his arm around her shoulder as Jackson and Grady took their places on either side of them. "I remember a time when we used to race to see which one of us could close the deal first."

"Once. We did that *once*. Almost a decade ago." When she'd have rather died than let her fellow cadets know she was a virgin. Her mission that night had been to find some guy she'd never see again, get laid and get it over with. Geez, that seemed like a lifetime ago.

"Has it been that long?" He looked down at her, his eyes twinkling mischievously and his teeth gleaming white.

She scowled. "Not long enough, I guess." Not if Mitch was still strutting around like a stag during mating season. He hadn't gotten any better since she'd transferred out of here for Langley.

Following the photographer's instructions, she scrunched in and placed a hand on McCabe's back. As she smelled his expensive sandalwood cologne her stomach dipped like she'd just rolled her F-16. Damn it. She refused to let him get to her anymore. He was the reason she'd asked to transfer out of Nellis. She'd moved hundreds of miles away trying to extinguish whatever she might have imagined she felt for him.

It had hurt to see him drinking and sleeping around after the divorce. She'd understood it. Up to a point. But she'd finally had to put some distance between herself and her buddy. Watching him become more and more callous had broken her heart.

Now she was just annoyed. Ever since she'd been stationed back in Vegas, resentment burned in her gut watching him continue to behave like a shallow serial dater. She'd hoped in time his flame of hatred for his ex would burn itself out. But she could see now that Mitch McCabe was determined to be nothing more than a walking booty call.

As the camera flashed, she forced a smile, and then stalked off toward the restrooms.

MITCH WATCHED HUGHES storm away. Something nagged at him. He was glad she was done with her internship at Langley, but his buddy had changed since she'd transferred back to Nellis last year. What was eating her?

While the bride and groom posed for more pictures with family, Mitch checked his Tag Heuer. Ten o'clock already. And a Friday night. How much longer was this shindig going to last? The only single woman in the room was that saucy redheaded friend of Jordan's. She'd flirted for a while before telling him she already had a boyfriend. Mitch's most important rule where women were concerned: no poaching. He sure as hell wouldn't do to some other poor schmuck what had been done to him.

Finally it looked as if the newlyweds were taking their leave. Jackson was acting like a lovesick fool, hanging all over his bride as if he had emphysema and she was oxygen. Even their buddy Grady—Mr. Control Freak—in an embarrassing public display of affection, had his wife, Lily, wrapped in his arms as he kissed her neck. Lily had wasted no time reeling the poor sucker in last year. And now that he'd returned from his tour of duty in Iraq Grady couldn't go two sentences at work without mentioning his wife.

When Hughes reappeared, Mitch sauntered over. He shook his head and rocked back on his heels. "Pathetic," he said under his breath. "First Grady falls on his sword, and now Jackson, slipping the matrimonial noose around his neck."

"Jordan and Lily aren't like Luanne, Mitch," Hughes said.

Pain stabbed his chest at the mention of *her* name. He couldn't believe Hughes had brought up his ex. Hughes knew, more than anyone else, how Luanne had destroyed him. "All women are the same, Hughes."

She glared at him, her hands curled into fists. "Are you saying *I'm* like Luanne?"

He blinked down at her. "No, but you're not really like…a woman."

Hughes's eyes narrowed to slits, and splotches of red appeared on her cheeks. "Not like a woman?" She ground the words between her teeth.

"Of course not." How could that piss her off?

"McCabe, you may be the most clueless male on the planet. If I didn't think it would upset Jordan, I'd take you outside right now and rip you a new one."

Mitch smiled. This was the Hughes he knew how to deal with. "You and what squadron?"

The bride and groom approached and Hughes gave McCabe a menacing glare before turning to accept Jordan's hug.

Jackson slapped him on the back and pulled him in for a one-armed hug. "McCabe, you dog. Your thirty days start today, buddy," Jackson announced.

Mitch stiffened. "What?"

"Remember last year you lost the bet and had to play monk for a month? You couldn't believe I was thinking of settling down with Jordan. And you once said if I *ever* got married you'd do without for another month." Jackson lifted one brow.

"Now, wait a minute." Mitch shook his head. Dread hit him low in the gut. "That wasn't technically a bet."

Jackson's mouth crept up in a slow grin. "So, you don't stand by your word."

"Of course I do!" Mitch's insides chilled as the legitimacy of Jackson's challenge settled over him like a bad case of the flu. He'd forgotten he made that promise to his buddy. Celibate for another thirty days? Last time he'd been somewhat prepared. Not because he was sure Jordan would give in and sleep with Jackson, but mostly because Mitch hadn't minded going without if that meant his buddy had a good time with the beautiful blonde. He shoved his hands into his pockets and turned on his heel, scowling at the ground. One glance at Hughes showed her smirking. The angry, hell-bent glint in her eye gave him the willies.

Jackson clapped him on the shoulder, bringing Mitch's attention back to the departing couple just as Jackson turned to his smiling bride and gave her a deep, promising kiss. The jerk did it just to rub in what Mitch would be missing.

Then, with one last wave, the newlyweds headed outside to their waiting limo. At the door, Jordan glanced over her shoulder and tossed her bouquet.

Mitch felt a small measure of satisfaction when the cluster of flowers slapped Hughes in the face and landed in her hands before she could duck for cover. "Damn it," she mumbled.

He chuckled. "Jordan should have been a bombardier with that kind of aim."

Hughes turned on him, her eyes blazing like laser-guided missiles. "You better get a wrist brace, McCabe." She gave him a surprisingly wicked smile. "'Cause for the next thirty days, your right hand's gonna be your best buddy." She marched out the door.

Geez, what had he ever done to her?

2

NOT LIKE A woman? Alex fumed. That was the third time McCabe had accused her of not being a woman. They were fighting words Alex could ignore no longer.

Of course, she'd strived her entire career to be treated equally. To not be thought of as a weak female. But still, it wasn't as if she was some genderless life-form. She *was* a woman.

And now that McCabe had gotten himself celibate again, this was the perfect time to show him just how true that was.

Within seven days, she'd formulated a plan and put it into action. Once Jordan returned from her Bahamas honeymoon, Alex had called to beg her help with a makeover. And Jordan hadn't hesitated when Alex explained her mission. In fact, she'd heard Jordan squeal before she shouted a resounding *yes!*

But now, after spending almost four hours being peeled, plucked and processed at a salon, and another three shopping at Jordan's favorite department store, Alex was rethinking her need to teach McCabe a lesson. "How do women *do* this all the time?" she whined as she tried to balance in the four-inch stilettos. "I'd rather shovel manure from my parents' stables."

"Hey, do you want to make Casanova McCabe pay, or don't you?"

"You're right." Alex squared her shoulders and stiffened her spine. "Suck it up, Hughes," she mumbled to herself.

All she had to do was picture the look of complete dismissal on Mitch's face when he'd said she wasn't like a real woman. If she had to break both her ankles trying to walk in these torture devices, she was going to make Captain Mitchell McCabe fully aware that she *was* a woman. A real, live, desirable female. And then she'd make him sorry he'd been born.

Jordan smiled and waved a hand. "I'm having fun. And you gotta admit the results are worth it." She turned Alex toward the full-length mirror in the shoe section of the department store. "Just look how the high heels and pointed toes elongate your legs."

Alex frowned at her poor feet jammed into the sheer red chiffon. She hadn't realized this famous shoe designer was a disciple of the Marquis de Sade. "Yeah, my legs will look real long sticking up in the air after I fall flat on my ass trying to walk in these things."

"Ain't gonna happen, girl." Jordan nudged her shoulder. "You just need practice. One foot in front of the other, heel to toe…"

Grumbling under her breath, Alex wobbled away, the muscles in her ankles screaming for mercy.

"Sway your hips just a little—no, not that much."

Alex adjusted her sway. This was ridiculous. She felt like a moron.

"Head up, don't watch your feet."

What? How could she make sure she didn't trip if she couldn't watch her feet?

"Good, now turn—slowly. Put one hand on your hip."

She was kidding, right? Did women really go through all this just to attract a man? She stuck a fist on her hip.

"Now come back toward me and watch yourself in the mirror. See how the new, subtle highlights in your hair soften your complexion and the new cut accentuates your cheekbones?"

Whatever. If Jordan said so. Alex smiled and nodded when Jordan asked her to try the walk again. And again. If she could survive *The Spa Dragon,* she could live through anything. Even—God help her—shopping. The facial had been kind of nice until the Dragon had told Alex her skin was "appallingly dry" and asked about her skin care regime.

Regime? Um…soap. Water.

The Dragon had looked as if she wanted to call security and have Alex thrown out until she'd agreed to buy the entire package of cleansers, exfoliators and moisturizers.

The pedicure and manicure had felt wonderful, but regulations forbade the bloodred nail polish that Jordan wanted her to get. The color would *so* clash with her combat boots and camo. She chuckled at the thought, lost her balance and teetered over, grabbing a stack of shoeboxes on her way down. An entire row of boxes and shoes came crashing on top of her as she landed hard on her butt.

Jordan rushed over. "Oh, my gosh, are you okay?"

"Nothing bruised but my pride." She tried to get her feet under her to stand.

"No, no, Alex! Not like that. Knees together."

"What? How the—" She clamped her mouth shut at Jordan's raised brow. "Okay, okay." Alex somehow managed to stand with her knees together and smoothed down the little black dress Jordan said was an essential piece in every woman's wardrobe. Of course, she'd said that about every item in the five shopping bags full of new clothes.

"Um…Alex?"

"Yeah?" She hobbled over to a bench and lifted a throbbing ankle onto her knee.

"We've got one more stop to make. Something I didn't think of until you—well, until a moment ago."

"Does it involve shopping? Do we *have* to?"

"Do you want to make him crazy, or don't you?"

Reserves of strength straightened her spine. "I want

that womanizing jerk brought to his knees." She rubbed the ball of her poor, tormented foot.

"Then follow me, Captain Hughes."

After paying for the shoes plus two other pairs of heels, Alex followed Jordan across the department store to the section devoted to undergarments. Good grief. The fancy pieces of nothing came in every style, size and color imaginable. Alex usually bought her plain white undies by the six-pack at the commissary. She'd never seen the point in spending good money on something no one would see anyway. But now...

She wandered around feeling completely overwhelmed until she spotted a violet-red thong and bra set made entirely from scraps of flimsy lace. Bet it would itch like crazy. But it seemed like just the sort of thing to drive a guy like Mitch absolutely wild. Not that she ever planned on him seeing it, but it would certainly help her *feel* sexy.

With a wicked grin, she found her bra size and took it to the dressing room.

3

Situation Report—Day Eight: tolerable.

If Mitch had known when he'd patted the sleeping brunette's butt and slid out of her bed two weeks ago that she'd be the last woman he'd have sex with for an entire month, he might have stayed the night for once.

Nah.

In his apartment off-base in Vegas, Mitch stood at the open refrigerator door staring at his options for dinner. He could handle doing without for thirty days. Last time hadn't been that bad even when he'd been on leave and partying every night on the Las Vegas Strip. All he had to do this time was avoid temptation.

Should be easy enough to do if he only went from work to home and back. He had plenty to keep his mind occupied. Air combat training. Classroom instruction. Changing the oil in his Jeep. Organizing his CD collection in alphabetical order.

And then there was always television…

He pulled his frozen dinner from the microwave, plunked it down on the coffee table, and sat back on his leather sofa. Peeling the plastic back, he poked around at what was supposed to be Salisbury steak while grabbing the remote. Let's see. Sunday night. He scrolled up the schedule of channels. Infomercial for the *Girls Gone Wild* DVD? No. Reruns of *Babewatch*—no! He punched the remote again. *Desperate Housewives*...

Screw this! A cold beer and a good game of eight ball was what he needed. Too bad Lily had Grady on such a short leash nowadays. But Hughes was usually up for a game. Even a bad-tempered Hughes was better than no Hughes at all.

Even though they'd texted and emailed, he'd missed her while she'd been stationed at Langley. With Jackson fighting in the sandbox back then, and Grady...well, even before he married Lily, Grady had never been much for having a good time.

He pulled out his cell and punched Hughes's number. After a couple of rings it went to voice mail so he left a message telling her to meet him at the officers' club for a game of pool. Then he shoved off his sofa, grabbed his keys and hopped in his Jeep.

As Mitch pulled up to the officers' club, he scanned the parking lot, but Hughes's Mustang wasn't there. Damn. Where was Hughes tonight? He pushed through the door and headed for the bar, ordering an appetizer and a draft of beer on tap. After finishing two beers and most of a plate of wings, he realized he'd been checking his watch for forty-five minutes. So, fine. She wasn't coming.

Reaching for his wallet, he paid his bill and strolled toward the pool tables at the back of the room. Empty. Didn't anyone else get out on a Sunday night? He chalked a cue stick, racked up the balls and had just lined up the first shot when he caught sight of a slinky red dress clinging to a cute little figure sauntering toward him. Her layered golden-brown hair blew around her heart-shaped face.

As his gaze traveled down her slim legs, his mouth went dry. He was a sucker for do-me stilettos like the ones she was gliding in.

He turned his back, hoping that ignoring the lady would get the message across, but he felt her come up behind him. He inhaled and some exotic perfume teased his senses and shifted his pulse into high gear. Damn it, where was his wingman when he needed her?

"You called my cell?"

Mitch spun so fast his cue stick hit the edge of the table, bounced up and almost whacked him in the face. "What the—" He looked the woman up and down, from her round pert breasts to her shapely legs, and back up to her face. "Hughes?" He choked on the word.

He squinted into her amber eyes. He'd never realized her eyes were more golden than brown. Or that she had such long lashes. Or that her lips were so…kissable.

He jerked away, bumping into the pool table. This was Hughes. His best bud. The grease monkey he called when his Jeep needed a new carburetor. Not some hot babe a guy thought about nailing. "Good God, Hughes, are you wearing makeup?"

Her lips tightened, and then she smiled and raised a feminine brow. "Alexandria."

"What?" Was that his voice sounding all hoarse?

"My name is Alexandria." She leaned closer, moistening her lips with a pink tongue.

"Alex—" he cleared his throat "—andria?" Was the AC broken? The room felt hotter than a Memphis summer. He tugged on his T-shirt. This just wasn't right.

Her brows drew together and she lifted a dainty hand with soft pink nails to cup his cheek. "Are you feeling all right?"

He flinched as if he'd been burned and scooted sideways, away from her scent and touch. But distance only gave him a better view of her incredible figure.

Mitch had seen her in a tank and shorts plenty of times, sweaty from a hard game of B-ball or a day in the Nevada heat under the hood of her Mustang. Now his imagination mutinied and envisioned her sweaty tank clinging to curves he'd never thought of her having before.

Damn, this wasn't helping his problem. He shifted his weight from one boot to the other.

She glanced around and sauntered over to the rack of cue sticks.

The way she walked, so…soft and sexy. God, had Hughes always had such a luscious ass? It looked just the right size to cup in his hands.

Snap out of it, McCabe. She was up to her old tricks. He'd punked her but good a few months ago and now she was just trying to get him back. They'd been pulling pranks on each other since their academy days. It would serve Hughes right if Mitch took her home, stripped off that dress and found out what those ripe tits felt like in his palms. But he wasn't about to break his word to Jackson. He still had twenty-two days of celibacy left. Maybe after that he could—

What was he thinking? He couldn't sleep with his best bud. That would just be too weird.

"So, you want to play or what?"

Play? A trickle of sweat dripped down his temple.

She gestured toward the pool table.

Oh, pool. Right. She wanted to play pool. "Uh, sure."

She turned and moved down the row of racks, inspecting the different sticks along the wall.

"You did this to yourself just for a practical joke?" he blurted out.

Her step faltered and she fell sideways into the cue sticks, sending them tumbling down.

Before he realized he'd moved, he caught her in his arms. She grabbed his shirt for balance as her ankles righted themselves. A horrified expression flickered over her face, and then was gone. He could feel her heat. Lust crawled over him. Intense. Unwanted.

She struggled out of his hold and stood on her own, smoothing her dress down over her hips. Her fingers slid over her flat stomach and down into the indentation between her pelvic bones, as if she was going to touch herself *there*.

He tried to swallow, but a hard lump blocked his throat.

A lieutenant appeared from behind Mitch and began picking up cue sticks and replacing them in their slots. "Is the lady with you, Captain?"

Mitch turned to the wet-behind-the-ears lieutenant. The guy was practically drooling, undressing Hughes with hungry eyes. Had Mitch flown through a wormhole in his Falcon this afternoon and landed in an alternate universe? He looked back at Hughes. "Uh…no."

The lieutenant grinned and edged close to Hughes. "Well, pretty lady, can I buy you a drink?"

Hughes scowled at him. "No."

"Aw, come on. Are you sure?" He put his arm around her waist and tugged her close against him.

The Hughes Mitch knew would've maneuvered out of the lieutenant's hold, grabbed his thumb and bent it back to the point of breaking for calling her "pretty lady." But this new Hughes grabbed the guy's shoulders with wide-eyed surprise.

"What's your name, sweetheart?" The kid crooned as his hand slid down Hughes' spine to the top of her butt. "I'm Drew."

Mitch's stomach cramped. He had a primal urge to crack the jackass's jaw. Hughes wouldn't actually go home with this kid. There were rules against fraternizing and he was pretty sure this guy was one of her students.

Hell, even if she was looking for some action, she could do better than smooth-talking Drew. But suddenly, that's all he could picture, Hughes in bed with Drew, his hands all over her.

Mitch stepped between them and folded his arms across his chest. "That's *Captain Hughes* to you, Drew. And if she needs a drink, I'll take care of it. Now get the hell out of here."

The lieutenant dropped Hughes like she was a live grenade. "Captain Hughes?" He stood at attention and saluted her. "Beg your pardon, ma'am." He spun on his heel and marched off.

Hughes turned to Mitch and arched a beautifully shaped brow. An enigmatic smile curved her lips. "Feeling possessive, McCabe?"

Her expression knocked the breath from Mitch's lungs. He'd never seen Hughes look at him like that. He grimaced. "Hey, I was just watching out for your career. Taking that lieutenant home would shred it."

Her smile dropped and she gave him a furious glare. "I told you when I met you, Lancelot, I don't need you or anybody else to look out for me."

"Apparently, you do," he snarled back.

She reached behind her for a cue stick and brandished it like a sword. "You're the one who's going to need protection by the time I'm through with you. Rack 'em, McCabe."

Mitch blinked. This was the old Hughes. "You're on."

She chalked her cue stick. "I'll even let you break."

"*Let* me?" With shaky hands and his pulse pounding in his temple as if he'd just climbed out of his cockpit, Mitch broke and called solids, but missed the first shot. Damn it.

She messed with his mind dressing up like this. He needed to get his mojo back, pronto, or she'd end up beating him.

Hughes was all business as she approached the table. She took her time examining possible shots from every angle, leaning over the edge until her heels lifted off the floor.

God, those heels. His gaze traveled from them to her delicate ankles and up her beautiful, smooth legs until they ended at the hem of her skirt. His imagination filled in where sight left off. He pictured his hands caressing their way up her thighs beneath the dress. What kind of panties would she wear? Would they be—

Holy crap, was he actually wondering about Hughes's underwear? What was the matter with him? He'd seen plenty of ladies in short red dresses. He'd taken dozens to his bed in all kinds and colors of under things.

But this was *Hughes*. In the twelve years he'd known her, he'd never seen her like this. He needed another beer. Hell, he needed ten beers.

Finally, she took her shot and sunk the ball. She moved around to the other side of the table and bent over to line up her stick for the next shot.

Mitch swallowed. He could glimpse the rounded swell of her breasts. His palms were sweating and, against his will, his body tightened. He'd never noticed how sexy her small breasts were. In fact, he hadn't thought about her actually *having* breasts since they'd first met. And worse, he could see the lacy edge of a red bra clinging to the soft flesh. She probably wore matching panties....

No matter how many quantum physics equations he went over in his head, he couldn't get ol' Mac to make a tactical retreat. At another time, with any other woman, he would have already suggested they go back to her place. But this was obviously what Hughes had planned. To torment him. What had ever made him suggest that idiotic bet to Jackson?

No, he should leave now and take care of his problem the only way left to him. And wouldn't Hughes just love it if she knew. After that smart-ass remark at the wedding...

Mitch swiped the back of his hand over his upper lip as he watched Hughes move around the table, bending over, the dress tightening around her cute backside. And she sank damn near every stripe. She finally missed the ten and Mitch got his chance to redeem himself. As she walked past him, she shrugged. "Let's see what you can do with your balls, McCabe."

Normally, Mitch would've laughed and maybe shoved her shoulder. The line was pure Hughes. But the woman who said it...wasn't. He took a deep breath and cracked his knuckles. He ran a hand through his hair and rechalked his cue stick. He took another deep breath while he studied the table. Then bent over and lined up his stick. He could do this.

Just as he drew back his stick and hit the cue ball, she came into his line of sight, bending over from the waist to fiddle with her shoe, and he scratched. Not just the shot, but the damn cue ball. Goddammit! Hughes had beaten him at eight ball before. But never because he'd been distracted by *her*.

In a temper, he rounded the table, closed the distance between them and grabbed her arm. "All right, Hughes! You've had your fun." He gestured at her dress. "But this isn't you."

She jerked out of his grasp, braced her hands on the edge of the pool table behind her and hoisted herself up to sit on it. She overshot the table and her dress hiked up, but he wasn't about to help her. He wasn't going near her.

With a toss of her head she crossed her shapely legs and the hem of her dress rose halfway up her thighs. "There are a lot of things you don't know about me."

"Oh, yeah? Like what?"

Her brows drew together and she bit her bottom lip.

Aw, man. Mitch had seen her do that a million times, but tonight it looked so damn sexy. Made him want to take her bottom lip between *his* teeth.

Her stubborn chin lifted and she folded her arms beneath her breasts. "I have a tattoo."

A tattoo? That was no surprise. Most guys in the military had something on their arm or—

"Down where no man has ever seen it."

He swallowed, images flashing through his mind. Would it be on her ass? Or maybe in the front, down low inside her little red panties…

"And I love to slip into a hot bubble bath at night."

Bubble bath? Hughes? Now he was picturing her wet, glistening skin, rising from a steaming tub. He blinked the image away. That was just what she wanted him to picture. "Next you'll be telling me you read romance novels and drink White Zin while you're in there."

"And what if I do?"

"Aw, come on, Hughes. Now you're just being ridiculous."

"McCabe, you dog." Major Sanders, a desk jockey in Civil Air Patrol, came up to them. "What do you think you're really going to do with this gorgeous woman, huh?"

Flanked by his two buddies, Sanders slowly moved over to Hughes, took her hand and bent to kiss the back of it. "Enchanté, madame," he drawled. "What brings you to our humble officers' club?"

"Oh." She graced Sanders with a sultry smile. "I'm interested in having some fun."

"Is that so?" Sanders glanced back at McCabe with a triumphant smirk. "You realize McCabe here has taken a vow of chastity?" He smiled into her eyes and his buddies laughed. "He can't do anything tonight but beat you at pool, darling."

Hughes's gaze darted to Mitch, uncertainty crossing her features. "He's not even doing that."

Mitch raised an eyebrow at her. Sanders wasn't a bad guy. A bit competitive, but mostly harmless.

Her expression hardened, and she turned back to Sanders, who still held her hand. "Buy me a drink, Major?" She jumped off the table and sidled up next to him.

Sanders grinned. "Sure thing, uh…you're going to think this is a line, but you look familiar. What's your name, darling?"

Mitch smirked. Sanders didn't recognize her.

"Alexandria." Mitch winced as Hughes tried fluttering her eyelashes. It appeared as if she had something painful in her eyes.

"What're you drinking, Alexandria?" one of Sanders's buddies asked.

"I'll take a JD, clean. And make it a double."

Sanders's buddy took off to get her drink.

"That's a hard drink for such a soft woman, Alexandria." Sanders's overt flirting knew no shame as his hands came to rest on her waist.

Mitch curled his fists to keep from interfering. What was it to Mitch if she slept with the guy? Or all three of them, for that matter. Besides, he knew good and well she could throw a mean punch. He'd seen her defend herself in worse situations. Like that night in Guam when he'd gotten revenge for the practical joke she'd played on him…

But she'd been in her camos then, and her steel-toed combat boots. He shook his head. Not his problem. Those heels of hers were lethal enough.

Mitch cleared his throat and tapped Sanders on the shoulder. "Uh, if you could move your little party somewhere else, I'd like to finish my game." He gestured to the shot he'd missed on the pool table.

"Sure thing, Monk-man." Sanders gave him a malevolent grin before backing away, with Hughes still in his arms.

Mitch clenched his teeth, but smiled back at Sanders. Let the guy gloat. He wasn't worth a formal reprimand, even if Mitch did long to kick his lily-white butt.

"Excuse me, *you* missed the shot, it's my turn." Alex couldn't tolerate Sanders's hands on her another second. She twisted out of his hold, stumbled in the heels again, and maneuvered herself across the table from Mitch. She tried to strike a sexy pose like Jordan had taught her. Shoulders back, chest out, one hand on her hip…

"You got back problems, *Alexandria?*" Mitch glanced up from retrieving his cue stick.

She opened her mouth to give a biting reply, but Sanders's buddy returned with her drink. "Thanks." She snatched it from his hand and downed the double shot in one swallow.

The guys had followed her around, and Sanders

stepped close and put his hand just below the small of her back where her thong strap was. She jerked and barely refrained from grabbing his thumb and twisting it from its socket. She wanted to make Mitch jealous, but if Sanders didn't keep his hands to himself, she was going to elbow him in the gut.

Mitch moved around the table, rubbing his bristled jaw. His facial hair was only slightly darker than the sun-bleached hair on his head. Just like the hair on his chest and arms, and...down there, too?

"Excuse *me,* Alexandria." He stood beside her, gesturing to the table. "Are you going to play or not?"

Appalled at her straying thoughts, she snatched up her cue stick, lined up her shot, and sunk the ball.

"Jeez, McCabe, you must have lost your balls in that bet to let a woman beat you," Sanders taunted.

"As a matter of fact—" Mitch drawled.

"Why don't you shut the hell up?" Alex straightened and spun to face Sanders.

Sanders barked out a laugh. Ignoring her, he still addressed Mitch. "You such a wuss you let a woman fight your battles now, too?"

Fury churning in her gut, she stomped her stiletto on Sanders's instep.

He hollered like a kid and bent over to grab his foot. "What the f—"

"Maybe next time you'll keep your wiseass comments and your hands to yourself."

"Hughes!" Mitch grabbed her arms from behind and

pulled her away. "Sorry, Sanders, you know what a temper Hughes has." Alex could hear the smile in his voice.

"Hughes?" Sanders glared at her while he held his foot. "This woman is Captain Hughes? I thought Hughes was—"

"Thought I was what?" She tried to launch herself at him again, but Mitch wrapped his arms around her chest and squeezed her to him. "Let me go." She struggled to be released.

"Calm down and I will," he said between grunts as he dragged her out of the club into the hot, dry desert air. "He isn't worth a demotion."

"Let him report me!" She quit struggling once they made it to her Mustang, but Mitch still held her tight, his muscled arms like a band of titanium around her rib cage.

"Come on, Hughes. You think he'll want to explain that injury to his C.O.?" Mitch's Tennessee drawl sent an ache straight to her core. Her chest rose and fell in deep gulping breaths, adrenaline still rushing through her veins. She became aware of Mitch's forearms just under her breasts, and she could feel his breath along her temple. Every inch of his hard body pressed against her back, enveloping her.

She looked down to study the masculine hands that had featured in more than one erotic dream these last dozen years. They were rough worker's hands, with veins that stood out when he had them clenched, like now. Slowly, she ran one finger along a vein, then took his hand and moved it up to cup her breast.

A deep moan escaped him and he leaned his head against hers. "Hughes, why are you doin' this?" There was an edge of desperation in his voice as his other hand moved to cup the other breast and he pushed his thick erection against her butt.

Desire and a deep sense of satisfaction spiraled through her. After tonight he'd never again think of her as just one of the guys. She closed her eyes and pressed back against him, covering his hands with hers. "You still think I'm not a real woman?"

"What?"

"At the wedding you said I wasn't a real woman."

"Aw, Hughes." Breathing harshly, he kneaded her breast over her dress and rubbed his fingers over one tight nipple. "I meant that in a good way." She har-rumphed, but his warm lips traveled down from her temple to the side of her neck, placing succulent kisses along the way. All else was forgotten.

Alex tilted her head to give him access to that spot behind her ear. But why stop there? Why not do what she'd wanted to do for so long? She spun in his arms, fastened her hands behind his neck and covered his mouth with hers.

At first he didn't respond, tried to pull away, but within a second or two he half growled, half groaned and took control of the kiss, sweeping his lips over hers, plunging his tongue in to lap inside.

At last. This was what she'd wanted for so long. His mouth moving over hers, his body pressed to hers. Her arms snaked around his shoulders, holding him like she'd never let him go. If it were up to her, she wouldn't. And he felt it, too. Whatever this was between them was strong. She'd known it for a long time. *Oh, Mitch. Yes.*

He yanked away, breathing fast, and wiped his hand over his mouth.

She stared into his baby blues, so full of passion. Yes. That's what she'd wanted. To make him notice her as a woman. To make him want her the way she—

"Hughes, I can't. Not now." He let out a long breath. "I gave my word. I still have three weeks."

As if the spell had been broken, she blinked, dropped her arms from his shoulders, and stepped back. With a strange sense of detachment, she noticed his fancy watch glint in the moonlight. The haze of lust dissipated and a chill settled over her. What had she done? How could she have let herself go there? She'd almost believed he could have feelings for her.

Of course he wanted to do her now. That'd been her goal with this prank, hadn't it? She shook her head, acknowledging in her heart what her mind had known all along. He was only interested because now he saw her as just another female to warm his bed.

She clenched her jaw and made herself snort. "I'm not going to sleep with you, McCabe." She folded her arms. Twelve years of frustration welled up inside her. "Not now. Not in three weeks. Not ever."

4

ON CADET FIRST Class Alexandria Hughes's first day at the Academy, her main goal was to make sure she didn't walk inside the halls with her eyes wide and her mouth hanging open. She couldn't believe she'd actually been accepted. To a small-town girl from the Texas Panhandle, attending the Academy was amazing, a dream come true and scary as hell. But she would rather have had all her nails pulled out one by one than show it.

After the swearing-in ceremony she stood on the field and watched all the other cadets saying goodbye to their parents up in the stands. Her parents couldn't afford the plane tickets or the time away from the ranch, so she headed inside. She understood why they didn't come, but it still gave her a pang to watch everyone else.

As she turned in to an empty hallway, she was

grabbed from behind, one hand clamped over her mouth while another guy pulled her hands behind her back and duct-taped them, then took her feet and carried her farther away, down another empty corridor.

She fought them, struggling against them, kicking, bucking, trying to bite the hand over her mouth. Her hat fell off, and her neatly pinned bun came undone. She knew what was coming if she didn't get away. But she wasn't getting anywhere fighting like this.

As hard as it was, she tamped down panic and quit fighting. Best to save her energy for an opportunity. They had to put her down at some point. But her heart was pounding triple time.

"Back in Memphis we call boys who pick on girls punk-ass cowards," a deep voice called from behind them. His smooth Southern drawl made it seem as if he were just having a nice conversation.

The upperclassmen holding her halted and switched their attention to the young cadet, and so did Alex.

With his arms folded across his chest, he leaned against the lockers with a nonchalance that bordered on cocky.

"What'd you say, boy?" one of her captors asked.

The Memphis madman pushed off the lockers and unfolded his arms. "I believe I called you punk-ass cowards." He raised a cocky brow to match his grin.

"Boy, you get the hell out of here and mind your own business," warned one, but his hold on her feet loosened as he spoke. This was her chance.

She kicked backward with her steel-toed boot and

heard the satisfying crack of one captor's knee, and his howl of pain. As he let go of her mouth, she turned and head-butted his nose as hard as she could. Yes! He was down.

She turned to see Memphis man had the upperclassman on the ground, beating his face to a pulp.

"Okay, that's enough. Hey!"

Finally Memphis looked at her, his dogged expression dissolving into a blank look of confusion. He glanced back down at the bloodied face he'd almost pulverized and then back at her. "You okay?"

Alex blinked at the pure beauty of the man. Even in his desert camo fatigues and a buzz cut, he was all golden hair and light blue eyes.

"Can you untape my hands?" She hated that her voice shook. It was just adrenaline kicking in, but she despised sounding weak in front of a classmate.

"Sure thing, darlin'." He flashed a smile that included dimples and Alex's insides kind of flipped. Pulling a Swiss Army knife from his boot, he cut the tape open.

Great. She hadn't even been here a week and her hopes of being treated equally were fading fast. How could she win the respect of her classmates if she couldn't fight her own battles? She had to be independent. She didn't want some guy with a savior complex running interference for her just because she was female.

As soon as the tape was cut she ripped off the rest of it, and started marching back toward the main building's foyer.

"Hey, wait up." He jogged to catch up to her.

"Don't ever do that again."

"Do what? Rescue you?"

She stopped and faced him. "First, you didn't 'rescue' me. Second, I don't need you to meddle in my problems. I can handle myself."

He glanced behind them. "Don't get me wrong, you did great, but I don't know about you handling two of them."

Despite herself, she shivered. "You may be right." She tightened her lips and folded her arms. "Thanks." Taking a deep breath, she lifted her chin. "But I need to take care of myself."

His brows rose. "Okay."

"Just remember that and we'll get along fine."

He nodded and held out his right hand. "Mitch Mc-Cabe." He was still smiling, still flashing white teeth and dimples. Despite the danger of what had just happened, his grin snuck past her carefully built defenses.

After a moment's hesitation, she shook it. "Alex Hughes."

As soon as she got back to her room, she sank down against the door with her arms around her knees and shook for half an hour.

SHE THOUGHT SHE'D made herself clear to Sir Lancelot then. She didn't need anyone. And despite her efforts to ignore the guy, it seemed like every time she fell behind on the obstacle course, or had to take an extra minute to get back up from falling down, he was there. Not offering a hand, but...just waiting with her.

She told him not to. To go on, leave her alone. She was fine. Finally, he seemed to get the message. Twelve weeks in, between the rigorous military training, the academic curriculum and the killer athletics program, she was exhausted and almost ready to quit. Though she'd die rather than admit it, the strain was getting to her.

After a worse than grueling day, when she'd failed at everything, she spent longer than usual in the shower, letting the hot water pound her sore muscles. When she got out, she wrapped up in a towel and padded out to the dressing room. She opened her locker and folded neatly in place of her panties was a pair of clean and pressed white men's boxer shorts.

She scanned the area, but she was alone. Someone had come in while she was showering and left again. Instead of creeping her out, the realization made her feel safe. Whoever it was, if he was going to harm her, he would've.

Rumor had it if a female cadet found a pair of men's underwear in their stuff she'd been officially accepted as one of the guys.

As she unfolded the shorts a playing card fell out. It was the king of spades. But the back was a picture of Elvis. The card was from a Graceland souvenir pack.

Alex smiled and shook her head. The king? Elvis? Memphis?

McCabe.

He was telling her she could do this. She was as tough as any man. And he had her back.

If she hadn't already, in that moment, Alex Hughes fell hard for Cadet First Class Mitch McCabe.

United States Air Force Academy, Colorado Springs, CO May 2000

ALEX STOPPED AT McCabe's door. Good, there was light underneath. She gave a brief knock and then let herself in. "Hey, Memphis?"

"Hughes! Thank God."

A warm glow filled her chest at the delight in McCabe's voice and face. To see her.

He sat with his ankle crossed over his knee, banging a pencil on a spiral notebook like a stick on a drum. "Is that pizza?"

"Our favorite, Mexican fajita with extra jalapeños."

McCabe tossed the spiral onto his desk, shot out of his chair and grabbed some barely used paper plates off the floor. "Let's eat." He set the pizza box on top of the spiral and seized the largest slice.

The man was too distracting in a plain white T-shirt just tight enough to hug the contours of his chiseled chest. And was she crazy to find camo pants sexy? She had to stop thinking about him like this. He had a girlfriend.

"You're studying?" She hopped onto his desk, set the box down and snatched a slice for herself.

He nodded. "Trying to memorize all those dates."

He gestured at the notebook under the pizza. "God, I hate all this history stuff. Who cares about some Roman emperor who ruled a thousand years ago?"

She leaned forward to pull the notebook out from under the box. Trying to read the chicken scrawl on coffee-stained notepaper was a challenge. "Is this Western Civ? I like that class. The stuff about the Hapsburgs…? Totally revealing."

He frowned. "Hapsburgs?"

"Yeah, women were just a means to gain power to them, the pigs."

"I must've slept through that part."

From the other side of the wall behind his desk came loud moaning and a rhythmic banging.

McCabe groaned. "My neighbor obviously has no anxiety about getting kicked out."

She scoffed. "And you do?"

"I have to get at least a ninety on the final exam or I'll flunk this class. If that happens, I'm out."

"That won't happen. We'll associate each date with something interesting to you."

He studied the pizza on his lap. "Hughes. If I can't hack it here, I can't ask Luanne to marry me."

She stopped chewing, horrified. "Marry you? You can't get married while you're in the Academy."

"No, but I can the day after we graduate. Why do you think they have that chapel here?" He grinned and excitement sparked in his gorgeous baby blues.

"McCabe. Seriously. You don't want to tie yourself

down at twenty-two. Don't you want to go off and see the world first?"

"Luanne and I've been going together since our sophomore year. She agreed to wait for me, so I can make something of myself. But I don't know if she'll wait any longer than graduation."

"Make something of yourself? What are you now, chopped liver?"

"Come on. You know what I mean."

Hughes's lips flattened. "All I'm saying is you're a great guy. Your girlfriend should love you for who you are."

McCabe gave her his cockiest grin. The dimples appeared out of nowhere and hit their target with deadly force. "I'm a great guy, huh?"

She lifted her foot to his shoulder and shoved. "Don't get your head all swelled up."

"Nah, that's the guy next door." He jerked his thumb toward the wall.

"Ugh." She tossed the rest of her pizza back on her plate. "Could've done without that image."

He chuckled and there was a comfortable silence while he finished his slice and she hopped off the desk and grabbed a soda from his roommate's minifridge.

"Hey, Hughes?"

"Yeah?" She popped the top off the can.

"How come you're not out having a good time tonight?"

"A good time? You mean, like, stand around waiting to see if there's a guy desperate enough by closing time to ask me back to his place so he can get his rocks off, and if I'm lucky he might be good enough to make sure I get my rocks off, too? That kind of good time?"

"Geez, when you put it that way…" He grabbed the soda from her hand and took a swig while he narrowed his gaze on her. "You'd be kind of cute if you'd fix yourself up a little."

She folded her arms across her chest. "Gee, thanks."

"I'm serious. Fix your hair, wear something nice and put on some makeup."

Alex bristled. "Why would I ever want to do that? So I can get groped by hormonal cretins?" She was comfortable in her old T-shirts and jeans. Her hair was cut so short there wasn't much she could do with it, even if she wanted to. The backward baseball cap hid it most of the time anyway. "I have to work twice as hard to get respect around here as it is. And besides, did it ever occur to you I don't want or need a man in my life? My mother slaves away cooking and cleaning for my dad and brothers 365 and you think they appreciate or respect her? Hell, no. A husband and kids is nothing but an anchor weighing down a woman, keeping her from becoming who she was meant to be."

McCabe held his palms up in surrender. "Okay, okay. I get it."

Alex inhaled a calming breath. Wow, that diatribe had been building inside her a long time. And poor Mc-Cabe didn't deserve all her built-up resentment. She let out her breath, feeling the anger leave with it. "Sorry for the rant."

"Forget it." He waved a hand. "So…you don't ever want to get married and have kids?"

She shrugged and took a sip of her drink. "Married maybe. When I'm old. Not kids. How could I be a fighter pilot and be pregnant? Or go into combat?" She shook her head.

His lower lip pushed out as he nodded. "Gotta admit, never thought of that."

Oh, those lips. *Luanne, you lucky girl.*

"What about you?" she asked. "I guess you and what's-her-name want a bunch of rug rats?"

He leaned back and clasped his hands behind his head, "I'd like four. She says two and then we'll see. I just want my kids to have everything I didn't have growing up."

"Four? Geez. I've got three brothers. You know how much laundry that'll take?"

He shrugged. "I can help with that when I'm home." He spread his hands out to his sides. "Besides, the world deserves to have these genes passed on."

Alex couldn't agree more. But she rolled her eyes. "You're so full of it."

He reached up and punched her arm. "That's what you love about me, though, right?" He grinned.

Love about him? What was not to love? Her heart hurt, but she made herself smile. "Damn straight."

"So, you gonna help me learn all these dates or what?" He grabbed another slice of pizza.

"Absolutely, Memphis. I got your back."

United States Air Force Academy Chapel, July 2003

IF THERE WAS a place in the ceremony where the minister asked the congregation if anyone knew of any reason why the bride and groom shouldn't get married, Alex decided she'd raise her hand.

Okay, so she probably wouldn't.

But she wanted to.

Don't do it, Mitch! She wanted to yell at him as she helped him straighten his tie. She finished and he turned to look in the mirror.

"Well, what do you think?" he asked, his gaze finding hers in the reflection.

He looked more handsome than a man had a right to in his dress uniform. She shrugged. "You clean up good." She made herself smile. "Hey, McCabe?"

"Yeah?" He grabbed his black leather belt and scabbard and buckled it around his waist.

"You know, there's no shame in changing your mind. Better now than after, right?"

He stopped fiddling with the buckle and gaped at her. "You've never liked Luanne."

"I don't even know Luanne." Alex swallowed, but soldiered on. "It's just so permanent. And you're both so young."

"Hughes. When you're in love, you just know when it's right. And this is right." He took her by the shoulders. "Luanne and I want the same things. Kids, a home, family."

Right. All those things she'd rashly told him she didn't want years ago.

But geez, Mitch was both blind and deaf when it came to Luanne. Alex doubted the girl had thought about much past the hearts and flowers and romance. She'd insisted on a huge wedding with all the bells and whistles. The cake, the flowers, the dress. And of course her parents provided it all, except the traditional rehearsal dinner last night. Which Mitch couldn't really afford. But he'd paid for her entire family, even distant relatives, to dine at the exclusive Penrose Room at the Broadmoor. Mitch was so hopelessly in love he wanted Luanne to have everything she wanted.

And that was what bothered Alex the most. This girl was a year younger than Mitch—only twenty-one, and she'd obviously, in Alex's admittedly biased opinion, been spoiled. Whatever she wanted, she got. Or else.

Mitch let go of her shoulders and picked up his saber. "Hughes, I think I know what's really going on here."

Alex drew in a deep breath. "You do?"

Did he know? She thought she'd hidden her feelings so well. All through the Academy, she'd tried to convince herself it was just infatuation. Besides, she wanted a career and her independence.

Mitch nodded. "You're afraid this is going to change our friendship. But it won't. Luanne understands we're just buddies."

Friendship. She let out her breath. Right.

He put his arm around her shoulders and squeezed. "And she knows guys need a night every once in a while to go out with their buddies for a beer and a game of pool."

Alex tried to smile and Mitch let her go to turn to the mirror and slide his saber into the scabbard. "Well, this is it." His eyes met hers in the mirror again. "I need you to be cool with this, Hughes."

She watched him in the reflection for a moment. His eyes shining with happiness and excitement. His heart so full of love and hope. Who was she to assume it wouldn't work out? Maybe Luanne was exactly what he needed in his life. And, above all, Alex wanted Mitch to be happy. He was one of the good guys. He deserved it.

So, she shoved down the malignant mass of churned-up emotions that threatened to ruin her best friend's most special day. If this was what Mitch wanted, this was what Mitch was going to have.

"Don't worry, Memphis." She clamped her hand on his shoulder. "I've got your back."

Near Randolph Air Force Base, San Antonio, TX, February 2004

ALEX WOKE UP instantly to her cell phone playing *Walking in Memphis*. "Hughes," she answered.

"Hey, Hughes, my wingman, come play some pool with me."

"McCabe?" He sounded drunk, but that wasn't like McCabe. Alex sat up and checked the time. "It's after midnight. We have flight training at 0600."

She heard him curse and what sounded like him fumbling his phone, then he said, "I forgot about training tomorrow."

"You...*forgot?*" How the hell did McCabe forget flight training? That'd be like Bush saying he forgot he was president.

"Shit, Hughes. You better come get me. I think I'm drunk."

"Ya think?" She was already pulling on her jeans. "Tell me where you are."

She was dressed and out the door in less than five minutes and found the pool hall off the interstate without too much trouble.

McCabe was sitting outside on the curb, his elbows on his knees, his head hanging down. It was cold and drizzly out, and he was getting wet. When she pulled into a parking space he looked up and Alex caught her breath.

She'd never seen such devastation in her friend's eyes. Even as he gave her a small smile. "Hey, Hughes." He stood and swayed on his feet and she raced over to catch him under his arm.

"Hey, buddy." She helped him walk to her truck.

His blond hair was disheveled and his desert camos were rumpled, but he still smelled of that expensive sandalwood cologne he always wore, and it pulled at her senses. She realized she'd been avoiding any close contact with him the last six months—since the wedding.

Contrary to Mitch's assurances before the wedding,

Luanne didn't understand. In fact, Alex was fairly certain Luanne didn't like her at all.

"Thanks for coming." He slammed his door and she went around to the driver's side.

"No problem." He'd already put on his seat belt and she snapped hers on before shifting out of Park.

They were halfway back to base before he said anything. She sure as hell wasn't going to ask questions. "Think I could crash at your place tonight?" He squeezed his eyes closed while he pinched the bridge of his nose.

"Sure thing." He must've had another fight with Luanne. But this one had to have been worse than usual.

Alex had gone out of her way to give the newlyweds space. To be on her best behavior. But McCabe's wife seemed to complain about everything. From what little he'd said, it sounded as if she spent most of her days either shopping for stuff they couldn't afford or complaining there was nothing to do.

Once they were at Alex's apartment she gathered up a spare pillow, blanket and sheets while McCabe hit the john. She was making up a bed on the couch when he came out.

She looked up from tucking a corner under the cushion and desire slammed into her like a tidal wave.

McCabe—Mitch had stripped down to his skivvies and undershirt. Black boxer-briefs had no business being on such a hard-muscled body. The combination was just too intoxicating.

Stop it, Alex, the man is upset. She tore her gaze away from his—whatever—and finished tucking the sheet.

"You didn't have to do that." He gestured at the made-up sofa.

"Shut up. It's done." She tossed him the pillow. "Good night."

"Good night, Hughes." He was staring at her as if he wanted to say more, so she stayed where she was. How she longed to close the distance between them, bring her hands up and smooth the deep lines from his brow and then soothe his anguish away with a kiss.

And how inappropriate was that? How could she blame Luanne for not liking her?

Alex made herself break eye contact and brush past him, but as she headed down the hall, she turned back. "McCabe?"

He turned to face her. "Yeah?"

"Things will work out, you'll see. I bet in the morning she'll call, and you'll apologize, and—"

"I caught her with another man in our bed this afternoon."

Alex actually felt her jaw drop open. She froze like that, unable to comprehend how someone could prefer any other man to Mitch McCabe. The stupid witch had him in her bed every night, got to lie in his arms, basking in his love. And that wasn't enough?

"Is she crazy?" She blurted the words out before she could stop herself.

McCabe gave a humorless laugh and plopped down into the love seat. His smile quickly disappeared as he stared straight ahead. "Can't blame her. The guy's the son of a Texas senator. He owns his own company and a lot of real estate in the area."

"Well, I sure *can* blame her!" Alex paced into the kitchen, flipped on the light and started making coffee. "She spoke vows to you, McCabe. And I don't think they said 'Till you find someone richer do you part.'"

He looked over at her then. "Yeah, but, I wasn't honest with her, either."

"You? No way you cheated on her."

The sorrow in his face softened. "You're so sure I'm a good guy."

She shrugged. "Of course."

He studied her a moment longer before turning his attention back to empty space. "I lied to her from the beginning."

For the second time tonight Alex stilled, frozen in the act of reaching for mugs in the cabinet. She saw Mitch in profile, saw his jaw muscle tick. His arm lay along the arm of the love seat and his fist was clenched.

"What about?"

"I told her my mother was dead."

"And…she's not?" She resumed getting down the mugs and then went for the sugar and creamer.

He shrugged. "As far as I know she's still drinking herself into a blackout every night, oh, and spreading her legs for whoever will buy her the booze."

Whoa. No wonder he wanted to pretend she was dead. "Okay. But that shouldn't be a deal breaker. *You're* not an alcoholic. You haven't moved your mom in with you, as far as I know, so why should it bother Luanne?"

"Ever since I told her the truth she's been...different."

"Because you lied? I think it's kind of understandable."

His chest expanded as he drew in a deep breath, then he exhaled and dropped his head back onto the love seat. "Don't you get it? She didn't know she was marrying some lowlife from the bad side of Memphis. I got into the ROTC and transferred to her high school. In a nice part of town. A respectable neighborhood. I don't even know who my father is."

"Mitch, Luanne should love *you*. No matter where you grew up, or who your parents are."

Still against the back of the sofa, he turned his head toward her. His baby blue eyes were bright with moisture. "I'm done with love, Hughes."

Goose bumps rose on Alex's arms at the hopelessness of his words, in his voice. She swallowed and busied herself with pouring them both coffee. "You can't forgive her?"

He narrowed his eyes and his expression hardened. "Could you?"

She replaced the coffee carafe in the coffeemaker and met his gaze. "No."

With a nod, he pushed off the love seat, stood and stretched, his arms extended high over his head. His stomach flattened and his rib cage broadened. "We better get some sleep." He rubbed his face with both hands and practically fell onto the made-up sofa.

"But don't you want—?" Before she could finish the question he'd turned on his side, his back to her. Alex stared down at the mugs of coffee in her hands. With a shrug she poured them down the sink and switched off the light.

For a long time after that, she lay awake in her bed thinking about the man lying on her couch. Wishing he were in her bed. Longing to know what it would feel like to be in his arms. And thinking guiltily that maybe now, just maybe, there might be hope for that dream to come true someday.

Nellis Air Force Base, Las Vegas, NV, 2007

"A toast," Mitch McCabe called out to the airmen gathered around the bar at the officers' club.

Alex lifted her bottle of Shiner's, looked around at all the friends she'd made the past year and tried to etch this image permanently in her memory. She was going to miss them, and this place.

After serving her tour of duty in Iraq, being stationed at Nellis had been like coming home to live in an amusement park. Especially when she'd learned that Mitch would be stationed here, also.

"To newly promoted *Captain* Alex Hughes," Mitch continued, his gaze finding hers across the crowd. "May her transfer to Langley be successful, and her exploits while she's there be numerous." He gestured to her with his tumbler of Jim Beam and then drank it down.

She tipped her bottle to him and then sipped her beer.

Alex refused to let tears come. She'd resigned herself to thinking of Mitch McCabe only as an old friend. A deeply troubled friend she couldn't help.

And she'd tried.

His bitterness after his divorce was only natural. But after returning from Iraq his womanizing had escalated to the point where Alex believed it fed his anger. It had become self-destructive.

Of course, Mitch didn't see it that way. The only time they'd ever seriously quarreled was the night she'd tried to have an honest discussion with him about it. Things had gotten pretty heated. After that night, she'd gone to her commander and requested a transfer. She couldn't stand by and witness what he was doing to himself anymore.

This change would be good for her. She needed to move on. A fresh start, a new environment, new friends. Maybe she could even find a man to love. She was twenty-six and she'd never had a long-term relationship. She'd like to know what it was like to have a boyfriend.

"Another toast," Major Grady called out and everyone raised their glasses and bottles again. "To Captain Cole Jackson, who's shipping out next week." Grady tipped his bottled water toward their friend Jackson. "Good luck in the sandbox, Captain."

Glasses clinked, and a few airmen called out, "To Jackson!"

Alex finished her beer, shrugged her way through the pack to Jackson and offered her right hand.

He shook it and pulled her forward for a one-armed hug. "Take care, Hughes," he said into her ear.

"You, too, Jackson. See you when you get back." Alex turned to find Mitch beside her. Their eyes met and held a moment before Mitch broke contact to shake Jackson's hand, telling him goodbye.

Then Mitch turned back to her. "So, what time's your flight?"

"It's early, around the buttcrack of dawn."

"Well, I'll come pick you up so you—"

"No."

He pursed his lips and folded his arms. "You're still pissed about our fight."

"No." She shook her head. "I just don't like goodbyes."

"But you asked for this transfer."

She shrugged. "It's a career move. An opportunity to work with Washington liaisons. I couldn't pass that up."

He cocked his head and raised a brow. "So, I guess this is goodbye."

"I told you. I don't like goodbyes. We'll keep in touch…it'll be fine." She extended her right hand.

He stared at her hand so long Alex thought he wasn't going to shake it. When he finally took her hand he yanked her to him and enclosed her in his arms. She felt his chin resting on her head. "I'm going to miss you."

Determined not to cry, Alex squeezed her eyes

closed. She'd told him she didn't want to do this. She pulled out of his arms. "Geez, McCabe, it's only a two-year assignment." She punched him on the shoulder. "I'll see you soon." And she turned and strode away.

5

Present day

SITUATION REPORT—DAY NINE: FUBAR.

How had his life gotten so messed up? Mitch slowly ran a hand over his face, then took a deep breath and headed for his jet.

"Eat my afterburn, McCabe." Hughes knocked into him as she passed him, striding across the tarmac to her F-16. Before she climbed up into her cockpit, she paused and smirked, then yanked on her helmet.

Mitch stopped in his tracks and blinked. This morning, in her bulky flight suit, thick combat boots and helmet hair, his old buddy looked nothing like the siren from the bar last night. And yet, all Mitch could think was, had she always had freckles? Before yesterday he couldn't have said. But her turned-up nose suddenly seemed sweet and sexy all at the same time.

And God help him, just being near her had him

fantasizing about the tightness of her nipples beneath his fingers, and the way her body had molded itself to his.

Snap out of it, McCabe.

This morning was the battle of the squadrons. They were teaching a tricky air combat maneuver to upper-classmen. With the Rolling Scissors, things could get hairy. Just the way he liked it. His adrenaline spiked as he climbed aboard his baby. There was nothing better than streaking across the sky in his F-16. It usually cleared his mind, brought life into focus.

After takeoff, the purple Nevada mountains on the horizon disappeared as he rolled over and headed for the Hoover Dam in preparation for simulated combat. Mitch loved seeing the endless expanse of unpopulated desert from this altitude. It seemed like a giant sandbox in which he got to play king of the world.

Suddenly he caught sight of Hughes's Falcon racing toward him. But it wasn't his buddy, Hughes, he pictured manning the cockpit. It was the woman in that dress last night.

I'm not going to sleep with you. Not now. Not in three weeks. Not ever.

Before he realized it, he'd missed his first turn, and then made it worse by overcompensating. That had never happened to him before. Not even as a rookie.

Hughes was forced to go off maneuver to avoid a crash. She bit off an expletive through the com.

"What's the matter, Casanova? Keeping it in your pants short-circuit your brain?"

Suddenly, Mitch hated his call sign. "You'd know more about that than me, Tex." He turned starboard to get back into position. "Let's try that again."

"That's what your last girlfriend said," Hughes taunted.

Mitch grinned. Good ol' Hughes. "Yeah, she couldn't get enough of me."

"Not much to get from what I've heard."

Like hell! He'd show her he was more than adequate in the size department. Just wait until— Damn it. Since when did he let Hughes psych him out like that?

"No comeback, Casanova?" He heard her malevolent chuckle through his headset.

Mitch cursed under his breath. Everyone on the com could hear their exchange. "I was just trying to protect your rep, Tex."

"Oh, yeah? How's that?"

"Didn't think you wanted everyone to know you were interested in my...uh, dimensions."

Ah, the sweet sound of silence.

"Get it right this time, Casanova." She was headed straight for him again. He concentrated on the maneuver, making the first turn with the precision he was known for. Then he "scissored" back and forth, crisscrossing paths with Hughes. Their wing tips passed within feet of each other. No question about it, she was good.

"Hey, Tex?" he called to her over the com as they got into position for their second demonstration.

"What?"

"Eat my contrail." He buzzed past her, flipped over and headed for the stratosphere.

"McCABE! IN MY office. Now." Commander Westland stood just inside the hangar, his arms folded, and his usually stern expression even grimmer. At least he'd dismissed the trainees before calling Mitch in for a dressing-down.

Marching in from the tarmac, Mitch kept ahead of Hughes, but she caught up to him at the hangar door.

"McCabe, you idiot! You could have been killed," she hissed.

Was he imagining it, or was that a quiver of concern in her voice?

Hands trembling, he gave one glance back to his Falcon. It was true. He'd screwed up. Bad.

Once in Colonel Westland's office, Mitch saluted and stood at attention.

"What happened out there this morning?" Westland never raised his voice. He didn't have to. His menacing tone could make the most hardened gang member cringe.

"Sir, I have no excuse," Mitch said. "I allowed myself to become distracted."

The colonel folded his arms, raised an eyebrow, and stared at Mitch. "You want to screw around, Captain

McCabe, do it on your own time, and with your own hundred-and-thirty-million-dollar aircraft, you got that?"

"Sir, I—" But what could he say? *I can't stop picturing Hughes in a red bra and panties, so I can't fly with her anymore?* Yeah, how fast could he say *dishonorable discharge?*

"Captain McCabe, I'm only going to ask this once. Do you have a personal relationship with Captain Hughes?" Westland asked.

"No, sir. We're friends, sir. That's all."

Westland leaned against his desk and stared Mitch down. "All right." The colonel narrowed his eyes. "Whatever's going on with you, get over it. Do I make myself clear?"

"Yes, sir," Mitch said.

Westland pointed at the door. "Dismissed."

Mitch blinked, saluted, then pivoted on his heels.

No way Westland believed him. Had the commander heard the rumor of their kiss? Was Hughes getting a dressing-down from Grady? That could ruin her chances for further promotion. Mitch couldn't let her take the fall. He'd make sure he talked to Grady before he left the base tonight.

After changing out of his flight suit, he met up with Hughes at the double doors of the mess hall. Mitch glanced at Hughes. She peeked at him.

"About the screwup today—"

"I told Grady it was my fault."

Mitch blinked. "And he bought that?"

Slowly, a grin spread across her mouth. "Partly."

Why had Hughes come to his rescue? Twenty-four hours ago, Mitch wouldn't have questioned her motives, but today, well, he saw her differently. She was…a woman. And he didn't need a woman doing him any favors. Women were devious, unreliable, out for whatever they could get.

"You shouldn't have jeopardized your promotion."

"Hey, that's what buddies are for, right?"

Were they still buddies? He'd never questioned that before. And he didn't like doubting it now. Hughes used to be just one of the guys. But hell, was she?

The thought of not having Hughes as a friend shook him. She was the only one who'd always been there for him. Avoiding her gaze, he headed for the lunch line like they did every day. As they passed tables, the room quieted.

Hughes slowed down and Mitch noticed airmen staring, following them as they grabbed lunch trays. Then he saw Sanders. The only guy in the room *not* staring at them. He was limping toward the door at a fast clip.

Hughes ignored the stares and piled her tray with her usual two sandwiches, bag of chips, apple, a bottle of tea and a bottle of water. Just one of the many things he'd always liked about her. No false declarations of needing to lose weight and eating only enough to keep a gerbil alive.

Didn't show on that figure of hers, though. His gaze

wandered down to her butt as she moved to sit across the table from him. Her ass was in prime condition. And so was the rest of her. The clinging dress she'd worn last night had left just enough to the imagination to drive a man insane.

"Hughes got catsup on her chest?" Their buddy Grady slid in beside Mitch and set his tray on the table.

Squeezing his eyes closed, Mitch realized he'd been staring at Hughes's breasts, picturing them as they'd been last night. He *was* going insane. But even more unbelievable, Hughes herself hadn't said a word. Since when did she miss a chance to make some remark at his expense? She was studying her sandwich as if it revealed the secrets of the universe. And was that a blush on her cheeks?

"I, uh. She... We—"

"This awkwardness wouldn't have anything to do with a certain lady in a red dress at the officers' club last night, would it?"

Hughes's gaze snapped up to Grady. "You heard?"

Grady grimaced. "I don't think there's an officer on base that hasn't."

Panic seized Mitch. That meant somebody had probably seen him kiss Hughes. And not just kiss, he'd groped her with about as much finesse as a horny teen.

"I don't listen to gossip," Grady said, giving a pointed look to Hughes. "Just wanted to warn you. You're not in the same squadron, but you still work together."

Mitch winced. They were both up for promotion. His

career was everything. And there was nothing more important to Hughes, either. At least, to the Hughes he used to know.

"I was just finally paying McCabe back for Guam," Hughes spoke up, and then took a huge bite of her sandwich.

Guam. That'd been, what, four, five years ago? He'd told a bar full of gamblers that Hughes was a nymphomaniac, after which she'd had to fight off a truckload of drunks. He and a few other guys on leave had jumped in and they'd all been hauled off by the MPs. Mitch almost chuckled.

Of course, he'd known Hughes's act last night had been a prank. And yet, he'd fallen for it. Damn, she'd probably had someone videotape the whole thing and post it on YouTube. An irrational feeling of betrayal crept up Mitch's intestines.

Not Hughes. Anybody but Hughes.

That kiss had been…real. At least, for him. And she'd acted as if it felt entirely real for her, too. Would she deceive him like that?

"You all right, McCabe?" Grady cut into Mitch's dark thoughts.

Mitch nodded. "Absolutely." He forced a grin. "Man, Hughes got me good. I should've seen it coming after losing that bet with Jackson." He ducked his head and spoke low only to Hughes. "You know, I could get you into bed if I really wanted."

Hughes snorted. "Yeah, right. Lucky for me you're... er, off duty for the next three weeks."

The derision in her tone pricked his pride. As he stared into her eyes, an electric charge zapped between them.

And suddenly he pictured her again as she'd been last night. Only this time she lay on his bed, her head in her hand as she beckoned him with a crooked finger...

Grady cleared his throat and the image shattered. "So, you ready for night maneuvers, Hughes?"

"Yes, sir." Hughes took a bite of her sandwich. "Looking forward to it."

So Hughes was going to start teaching night maneuvers? That meant she'd be on night rotation for at least three weeks. With his day schedule, he'd never see her. Maybe that was a good thing.

He glanced at his watch, shoved his tray away and stood. "Got a class." He nodded at Grady and turned to go.

"McCabe!" Hughes called after him, and he glanced back.

"Don't forget. My place. This weekend."

Her place? He blinked as an image of them rolling across her bed shortened his breath. Had she changed her mind about—

"I'll bring my extra rollers and trays," Grady said.

Oh yeah. Her new house. They'd promised to come help paint. "I'll be there." He shook his head. "Jeez, Hughes, you wear a dress once and turn into a nag."

He'd taken three steps when an apple thunked him on the back of the head.

Damn, that felt good.

ALEX'S HANDS SHOOK as she reached for her sandwich again. She could feel Grady's stare on her as she took a bite.

"Just a prank?" he said quietly.

"Good one, huh?" she answered around the food tucked in her cheek.

She took another bite of her sandwich as he continued to watch her with the intensity of a raptor closing in on its prey.

"What?" She slammed her sandwich down. "You gotta admit he deserved it, after the hundreds of women he's left in his wake."

Grady merely raised one brow.

"You don't seriously think I have the hots for Mi— McCabe?"

His eyes widened. "Never thought of that."

Great. Now she'd planted the idea in his head.

"We're friends. That's all."

He picked up his soup spoon. "Whatever you say."

Alex shot to her feet. "Come on, Grady. You know me."

Seemingly unaffected by her fuming, he shrugged and ate his soup.

She unclenched her fists and took a deep breath. She protested too much. And Grady knew it.

As long as no one else did.

6

SITUATION REPORT—DAY TEN: under control.

Tuesday afternoon around five, Mitch found himself in Hughes's office, leaning against the doorjamb as she finished filling out forms.

After shoving a stack of papers in her out-box, she glanced up. "You look like crap."

"Thanks, I'm trying something new."

She shook her head and clicked her tongue. "Celibate less than two weeks and it's already giving you blood-shot eyes and dark circles."

Yeah, that must be what was bugging him. He hadn't slept well—or much at all—the past couple of nights. He'd twisted in his sheets, confused and...unsettled. But he'd rot first before admitting that. He grinned, pushed off the doorjamb and came into her office. "Think how the ladies will love to soothe my fevered brow."

Shaking her head, she suppressed a smile. "You're

hopeless." Getting to her feet, she grabbed her jacket and briefcase and took a step toward the door.

"Thought we'd grab a couple of beers."

She stopped in her tracks and stared up at him, her expression inscrutable. "Uh, I can't. The Mustang. Needs new brake pads."

"Great. You provide the Shiner Bock and I'll bring the pizza." He shoved his hands in his pockets, spun on his heel and sauntered out the door.

AN HOUR LATER Alex heard Mitch's Jeep pull up and squashed the urge to run into her house and change clothes or wash off the grease. This was McCabe. He'd seen her greasy before. Once he'd even held her head while she puked up her guts. What was the big deal?

But the truth was, greasy or not, she didn't want to be around him right now. Curse her slow brain this afternoon. Any excuse would've been better than working on her Mustang. They always helped each other with car repairs.

Mitch's boots appeared at the edge of her vision. "You started without me?" The aroma of pepperoni and melted mozzarella drifted to her nostrils.

Alex rolled out from underneath her 'Stang and took his waiting hand to pull her to her feet. But Mitch didn't let go. His gaze lowered to her chest and remained there.

She looked down. What? She was wearing the same thing she always wore when they worked on their cars.

Ratty jeans and an old T-shirt that had once been her brother's. And no bra.

This had never been a problem around Mitch before. But between the cool fall air and Mitch's gaze on them, her nipples had tightened to the point of pain. *Act normal, Hughes.* But her breathing was erratic and her heart was pumping hard.

Mitch's Adam's apple fell and rose as he swallowed, and then he licked his lips. He finally met her eyes, and she could read the hunger mixed with confusion in his. Briefly, she considered kissing him again. But if she did, she might not stop this time. *Uh, yeah,* you *didn't last time.*

She tugged her hand from his grasp. "Let's eat." Slamming into her house, she headed for her bedroom, put on a bra and tugged on a thick sweatshirt, telling herself the sun was going down and the air was cooling. Then, grabbing the six-pack of her favorite Texas beer from the fridge, she joined Mitch on the porch for pizza.

"So, how're your rookies?" Mitch finally spoke around a bite.

Alex nodded. "Not bad. Got the usual too-cocky-for-his-own-good recruit."

Mitch chuckled. "Nothing wrong with having confidence."

Alex stared at Mitch's beautiful smile and felt her own mouth lifting at the corners. For a second, they were once again buddies sharing a pizza and repairing a car together like they had plenty of times over the years. Then his smile faded. "Alex…?"

She shot off the porch step. "Better get to work before we lose the daylight." She wiped pizza grease on the front of her jeans and practically dove for the safety beneath the car.

"Damn it." She could kick herself. She'd left her tools out there.

"Hurt yourself already?"

"Make yourself useful and hand me that ratchet."

She heard shuffling and metal clanking and then he was wiggling under the Mustang beside her, his body achingly close. He'd showered and smelled of clean, masculine soap. With the car up on blocks there was plenty of light and room to see clearly. She was acutely aware of the hard planes of his chest under a tight T-shirt. Of his breath hitting her cheek.

This was ridiculous. They'd worked beneath their various cars and trucks dozens of times.

"Here you go." The ratchet hit her waiting palm with a sure but gentle slap.

"Thanks." Did her voice sound breathy? Would he assume she was just working hard on loosening the brake pad? She closed her eyes and tried to take in a deep slow breath, tried to force her body to regain some semblance of control.

"Is it being stubborn? Want me to try it?" Mitch asked, his voice low and close to her ear.

What she wanted was to roll over and nuzzle into his

broad shoulder and flatten her hand on his taut stomach, and maybe inch her fingers slowly under the waist of his jeans, and farther down to cup him and see if he was as hard as she was wet.

"Hughes?"

Alex jerked and her eyes popped open, the fantasy burst, leaving an evaporating trail of misty longing. "I got it," she snapped.

"Geez, fine. I'll work on the rear pads." He scooted away, leaving her alone with her miserable, throbbing need.

For the first time ever she wished she could just drive down to the Strip, find some anonymous guy and relieve her itch. Because even if Mitch weren't honor bound to be celibate the next three weeks, there's no way she'd ever do the mattress mambo with Casanova McCabe. It would kill her to be just another notch on his joystick.

But she was too old for one-night stands and predawn walks of shame. If she started an affair with someone at this point in her life, it would be because she was serious about the guy.

By sheer determination, she shoved her desire down into the deep place inside where it usually resided, and concentrated on brake pads.

Mitch started replacing the rear brakes and they fell into a natural rhythm of passing tools back and forth, and communicating without words, a camaraderie that'd been built over years of having each other's backs.

A dozen years of trust, companionship and loyalty.

No way she'd give that up for a night of sex. Some people might be capable of being friends with benefits. But she knew, way down deep in the truest part of herself, if she ever slept with Mitch, she'd want the whole shebang. His heart, his soul, and, yeah, at this point, his kids.

7

Situation Report—Day Fourteen: he had no freakin' idea.

For the second time in a week, Mitch parked his Jeep in front of Hughes's newly purchased house. He shoved the keys in his pocket as he jumped out. Waves of heat rose from the black pavement. Hughes *would* pick the hottest day in September for this painting party. She'd better have plenty of beer stocked.

Normally, he'd have been looking forward to a day like this. Barbecue, beer, maybe some foosball and air hockey later.

But even that couldn't entice him. He didn't want to be here.

It'd been a strange week. Everything seemed normal between him and Hughes. But something felt…not right. Strained. He'd tried to get their friendship back on track by offering to help with her Mustang. But that had been just as disastrous as the air combat maneuver the day before.

Come on, McCabe. Shake it off.

The other day he'd been so focused on the weird vibes with Hughes he hadn't really noticed the house. Her new home was small and old, probably built around the 1950s or '60s. An old tree shaded the green lawn. Not something one typically saw in Vegas.

Mitch could tell the front yard had recently been landscaped with trimmed shrubs and brightly colored flowerbeds. Hughes—or someone—had put a lot of sweat equity into the curb appeal. If he'd ever once dreamed of the perfect family home as a kid, this would have been it.

Now it just made him want to jump back in his Jeep and head for the nearest bar.

The front door was open and he let himself in. The living room had the same homey atmosphere the front lawn had promised, with a comfy sofa, a warm area rug and a club chair all grouped together. This front room had already been painted a soft buttery cream color. A week ago, he would have doubted this house would suit Hughes. But now he wasn't so sure.

Before he was tempted to go check her bathroom for romance novels, he strode into the kitchen and grabbed a beer from the fridge. Grady was on a ladder painting the wall above white cabinets.

"'Bout time you showed up," Grady grumbled without ever looking away from the wall and his roller.

"Am I late?" Mitch made a show of checking his watch and then popped the cap off his bottle.

"We've been here since 0800." Grady finally looked down at him and then descended the ladder. "But I saved the master bedroom for you." He shoved a paint can and a clean roller into Mitch's arms.

"Where's Hughes?" No way Mitch was painting a bedroom with Hughes in it.

"Out back. Making lunch."

"Mitch! You're here." Lily swept into the kitchen and hugged him. "Oooh, your aura is cloudy." She cupped his cheek. "Poor confused guy. You need a tarot reading from my friend, Sun—"

"Lily, sweetheart," Grady cooed as he came up behind her and wrapped an arm around her waist. "The last thing McCabe needs is your sympathy."

"But, Ethan, if it weren't for Mitch giving you my apology card, we might not have found each other again. He's the one who called me when—"

"Okay. Okay." Grady smiled warmly at his wife. "Whatever you want, baby."

"Oh, Ethan." When Lily put her arms around Grady's neck, lifted onto her tiptoes and started kissing the guy, Mitch took that as his cue to leave. He could only stomach so much saccharine.

As he stepped around the couple, he could see through the sliding glass door into the backyard. His hand halfway to the door handle, he came to a dead stop.

Hughes was standing in front of a fancy new propane

grill wearing cut-offs and a backward ball cap. She'd spilled paint on a faded, too small T-shirt that hugged her tiny curves. She was flipping burgers and, as he watched, she wiped her temple on her T-shirt and managed to smear white paint on the side of her face.

God, she looked cute.

Mitch choked on the thought. Cute? Cute was for puppies and kittens. Not women. And definitely not women he was usually attracted to. He liked 'em brash and bold, bodacious and big-busted. Not necessarily in that order.

As if she sensed his stare, she turned and caught sight of him standing there like a clueless recruit, his hand paused in midair. She frowned, pointed to the nonexistent watch on her left wrist, and motioned for him to come outside.

Mitch stepped out and heat blasted him like jet-engine blowback. An empty pool teased him with possibilities. He pictured it filled with sparkling turquoise water beckoning him to escape the heat.

"Now you decide to show up?" Hughes berated. "Just in time for lunch?"

"Hey, I never said what time I'd be here." The landscaping in the backyard was a work in progress. *Work* being the operative word. Mitch shuddered at the thought of buying a house. The upkeep and repairs seemed like something for dopes chasing the ever-elusive American Dream. After the divorce, he'd put that delusion out of his mind.

"Most of the painting's already done." Hughes had turned her attention back to her grill. "But if you want one of my famous Texas burgers, grab a roller and get to it, buddy."

Mitch shrugged. "Eh, I'm not hungry." He took a swig of his beer and then couldn't stop a grin.

Hughes swatted him hard with her long-handled BBQ spatula. "Git!"

"Ow!" He rubbed his arm. "You got grease on my best Hawaiian shirt!"

"That'll be the least of your problems if you don't get painting," she threatened.

Mitch grinned, went back inside, and met Jackson and his new bride in the hallway. Seemed like they were getting more paint on each other than the walls. They broke apart once they caught sight of him.

Jackson cleared his throat and shot him a sheepish grin. "McCabe. How's it going?"

"Apparently, I'm late."

"Really? We hadn't noticed." Jackson reached over and patted his wife's behind.

"Cole!" Jordan yelped and swatted his hand away, but she was smiling and snuggled up against the guy. Jackson lowered his head and began raining kisses all over her face.

Mitch was quickly approaching his breaking point. Any more lovey-dovey and he was outta there for good. "Please. Don't mind me."

The Jacksons barely noticed his departure.

Mitch took the paint can, tray and roller into the master bedroom and got to work. Or, at least, he meant to. Most of the furniture was shoved to the middle of the room, covered by a plastic sheet.

With a quick glance out the bedroom door first, he gingerly lifted the plastic and inspected the books stacked on Hughes's bedside table. Damn. She'd punked him again. There were mostly aviator biographies, combat and war nonfictions, and a political humorist's book, but no bare-chested men or couples clinching.

Good to know he at least knew her that well.

His gaze moved on to the top of a long dresser and he lifted the plastic. Framed photos of her family back in Texas. Her brothers and their wives and kids, her parents. And one of her as a teen on a horse. She wore a white cowboy hat, a white Western shirt with fringe along the yoke, and a huge grin as she held up an oversize gold belt buckle.

He knew she'd grown up on a ranch outside Amarillo, and he vaguely recalled she'd mentioned barrel racing in the rodeo as a kid. She must have been pretty good if she won the buckle.

She looked funny with long curly hair past her shoulders, but other than that she looked the same.

His ex had had a big, warm family, too. But that was where the similarities ended.

Would Hughes's family like him? Luanne's family had taken him in as one of their own. So much that Luanne had accused him of marrying her for her family, and not her. It wasn't until this moment that he considered whether that might actually be true. Well, if it was, the relationships had ended with the divorce. After that, they'd treated him as if he had the plague.

He couldn't blame them. They'd just been loyal to their daughter. Alex's family would stick by her, too, he imagined. They looked like a close-knit bunch.

"Snooping, McCabe?"

Mitch jumped and spun to face Hughes standing in the doorway. "Why'd you leave?"

"What?" Hughes's brows crinkled.

He lifted the framed photo. "You had it so good. Why give all that up for combat and soldiers' rations?"

She came into the room and took the frame from him, studying the picture. "Geez, was I ever that young?"

"You look happy, though."

"Yeah, I was. Mostly. You know. Families can be difficult."

"What's difficult? Nice house. Two parents. You even had a horse."

She put down the picture and pierced him with a penetrating gaze. "My mother wanted me to be like her. Little Suzy Homemaker." She raised a brow and grimaced. "Can you see me wearing an apron and oven mitts, baking pies?"

"No." He picked up the photo with her mom and dad and dropped onto the plastic-covered bed. "But at least your mom made a home for you."

She shrugged. "That's true. But at the time, all I saw

was the drudgery. Cook and clean and wake up the next day and do it all over again. If I'd married some neighboring rancher like they all wanted, that's what my life would've been."

He nodded. Had his mother seen her life as drudgery? Living in that dilapidated trailer and having to take care of him? Was that why she'd drunk herself into a stupor every night?

"Your mom…it was bad, huh?" Hughes asked as if she'd read his thoughts.

He stood and returned the photo to the dresser, then picked up a stick and stirred the can of paint. "Oh, you know, I did okay."

After a moment of Hughes not saying anything, Mitch looked up from pouring paint. She was watching him with such intensity, if he'd been a kid he would've squirmed. "What?"

"You always do that."

"Do what?" He smiled and poured the paint into the tray, reading the sticker on the can. "Celestial Celery? Come on. Why don't they just call it green?"

"Deflect. Change the subject. Anything but talk about your childhood."

Mitch shrugged and shook his head. He'd always regretted going to her that awful night his marriage ended. Letting her see him weak and sniveling. No way he was going to expose anything more. "I was a kid, I went to school." He spread his hands out to his sides in a gesture that said that's all there was. His smile was getting more difficult to maintain under her penetrating gaze.

She folded her arms and raised a brow. "You can talk about it with me, you know."

"Jeez, Hughes." He picked up the roller and dunked it in the tray of paint. "What are you, my therapist all of a sudden?" He tried to fake a laugh.

"You told me your mom was an alcoholic—"

"Just drop it, all right?" He jabbed the tray of paint with the roller, splattering paint, and then attacked the walls with it.

He heard her suck in a deep breath. Here it came. With Hughes's temper, she'd tell him off before marching out.

But all she said was, "I came to tell you your burger's ready."

Mitch blinked at the spot where Hughes had been standing. He took a step toward the door. Ready to leave, to drive off and forget all about the stupid painting party. But he'd be damned if he'd retreat like a yellow-bellied coward. So, he dipped the roller in the tray again and slapped paint on the walls as if they were the enemy.

The physical labor released the tension, but the mindless repetition of the job gave him too much time to think.

Not too many people, male or female, he'd spend his day off helping. He could name his buddies on half a hand. And he'd never ask them for anything. He didn't like the feeling of being in someone else's debt. Too many times he'd watched his mother humiliate herself for a loan that would only be paid back one way.

Forty-five minutes later he'd finished all four walls and his stomach was growling. He cleaned up and made his way to the kitchen.

He caught sight of Hughes at the front door hugging Jordan and Jackson. "Y'all come back next weekend and we'll swim. I should have the pool cleaned and filled by then."

"Let's do brunch tomorrow, just us girls," Jordan suggested. "And then go shopping. Lily wants to look at cribs."

"Sounds fun," Hughes answered as she waved them off.

Lily was pregnant? They sure worked fast. Grady had only been home from Iraq a couple of months. And looking at cribs sounded fun to Hughes? Since when was she interested in babies?

When he'd asked her about buying this house, she'd scoffed and said something about turning thirty and being tired of apartment life.

Mitch took in the rest of her house. Curtains on the front windows, a dining table with place mats. Candles and knickknacks on the small fireplace mantel, and kitchen towels that matched the place mats.

Were these somehow signs of a lifestyle change? Was she getting ready to settle down and have a family? Her career was more settled now. Was it that guy she'd mentioned dating while she was stationed at Langley? That SEAL?

Feeling a little off, he rubbed his empty stomach.

Before Hughes could throw him out, he headed for the patio where Grady and Lily were. Lily was leaning against Grady and he was rubbing her back with one hand and cupping her flat belly with the other, murmuring something in her ear. She nodded.

"Thank y'all for helping," Hughes said from behind Mitch. "But, Lily, if I'd known you were pregnant, I would have insisted y'all stay home."

"Oh, no. The paint's nontoxic. I'm a little tired, but nothing a nap won't cure."

Grady and Lily said their goodbyes, Grady shaking Mitch's hand, Lily hugging him. Hughes walked them out.

A paper plate with two juicy burgers loaded just the way he liked them, a bowl of chips, a bowl of barbecued beans and two icy cold drinks sat on a battered picnic table. Mitch gratefully swung a leg over, grabbed a burger and dug in.

When Hughes came back out she was carrying a large bottle of some sort of cleaner. Without a word to him, she made a beeline for the garden hose, hooked it up to a power washer and pulled the washer nozzle down the steps with her into the empty pool.

She was giving him the silent treatment? Just like a woman. She wouldn't tell him to get the hell out, but she wouldn't get over their stupid spat either. He stopped chewing. He sounded like a married man talking about his wife!

No. That was ridiculous.

He slammed up from the table and stalked over to the pool's edge. He had to yell above the motor of the power washer. "Just what is your problem anyway?"

She eyed him, shut off the washer, slopped some cleaner against the side of the pool and started scrubbing with a brush. "I don't have a problem. Did you already finish the bedroom?"

He stuck his hands on his hips. "Yeah."

"Well, thank you for helping out. Don't feel like you have to stay."

Mitch hesitated. Did this mean they were good now? She wasn't mad anymore? Just last week he would've known exactly what that meant.

Screw it. He kicked off his shoes, stripped off his expensive watch and joined her.

She stared at him a moment, then gave him a half-hearted smile. "What about your best Hawaiian shirt?"

He shrugged and grinned. "It's my second best."

She gave him that look she'd been giving him a lot lately. The one that said, "You're hopeless, McCabe." Then she tossed the brush at him.

He caught it with a grunt. While he scrubbed, she rinsed with the power washer. After making his way around one side of the pool and achieving a hefty sweat, he straightened, wiping his brow with the back of his hand.

Cold water sprayed his shoulder and he spun around.

Hughes's mouth gaped open. "I'm sorry. It was an accident." She tried and failed to suppress a snicker. "You should see your face." She burst out laughing.

He charged at her.

"No," she called to him as he advanced. "The nozzle just got away from me, I swear." Grinning widely, she dodged his grasp and turned the sprayer on him full force, soaking his shirt. She screeched as he made another grab for it and fought him for possession.

She was laughing wildly as she struggled in his arms, no match for his strength. But he was no match for her soft curves and tiny waist as his hands slid over her body. One minute they were fighting for control of the nozzle, the next he yanked her against him and covered her mouth with his.

Like the last time they kissed, his world clicked into place. Everything felt right. Her lips moved with his in perfect rhythm, her tongue teased his. Her body fit into his, soft and round where he was firm and flat. His cock pressed against her stomach and he cupped her bottom to hold her even tighter against him.

Then her mouth was gone. He continued pressing soft kisses down her jaw and neck and back up behind her delicate ear, until he realized she was trying to pull away.

Breathing heavily, he let his hands drop from around her hot, lithe body and stepped back.

Her lashes were spiky wet, and she was biting her

lower lip. She held her hands in front of her, palms out, as if she couldn't bear to touch him. Her golden-brown eyes gazed up at him with, what? She looked scared. Vulnerable. He'd never seen Hughes look like that.

"What's happening to us, Hughes?" His voice shook, for the first time he could remember.

"I—I don't know." She dropped her gaze and folded her arms around herself. "Maybe we can't be friends anymore."

No. He couldn't lose Hughes. She was his best friend. If she didn't want him kissing her, he'd stay away. He'd get over this…infatuation, or obsession or curiosity. Whatever it was, he could lose it. But he couldn't lose Hughes.

With a gut-wrenching noise he turned away and heaved himself out of the pool. He scooped up his shoes, grabbed his watch and stalked out to his Jeep, screeching his tires as he pulled away.

8

EXACTLY ONE WEEK later, Alex brought the last, lone steak inside and set it on the kitchen counter.

Mitch's steak.

He hadn't shown up. Hadn't called or texted. He'd just blown her pool party off.

Lily came up beside her carrying a tray of empty glasses. "I know you don't believe in my premonitions, but I have a feeling something good will come from all this."

Alex peered behind Grady's wife to make sure all the other guests had gone. She refused to discuss anything sensitive in front of her colleagues from the base or any new neighbors. Forcing a smile, Alex said, "Something good from my pool party? It was fun. I'm lucky to have such great friends."

Lily put her hand on her shoulder and gave her a look that, back in Texas, would have meant, "Bless your little heart, but you're slow."

"Good steak, Hughes," Grady said as he came up behind Lily and wrapped a protective arm around her waist.

"I was telling Alex that things will be okay between her and Mitch soon, I just know it."

"What about Alex and Mitch?" Jordan asked as she and Jackson stepped into the kitchen carrying their ice chest.

"Nothing!" Alex tossed the steak into her sink, switched on the disposal, and shoved the hunk of meat down with the grill tongs. "I'm sure he's plotting his next outrageous prank right now."

As she glanced around at her company with a flawlessly nice smile, every one of them looked appalled, and she realized she was still shoving the meat down into the disposal as she talked.

"That was perfectly good tenderloin, Hughes." Jackson pointed at the sink.

"Come on, honey, it's late." Jordan grabbed her husband's arm and dragged him toward the front door.

After that there was a mass exodus. Jordan assured Alex they'd get together soon, and Lily whispered something about watching out for sea animals to Alex as she hugged her goodbye.

Sea animals? Did Lily think Alex was going to be injured by a killer dolphin? In the middle of a desert? That girl was a sweetheart, but she was certifiable.

Alex waved them off, then closed her front door and leaned her forehead against it.

Did they all know how she felt about Mitch?

Damn him, anyway. She hadn't seen him since that disastrous, wondrous kiss in the pool. But she'd assumed it was because she'd started teaching night maneuvers this week and he was still teaching during the day. Now she wasn't so sure. Would he throw away their friendship so easily?

Rolling to rest her back against the door, she closed her eyes and played the kiss over again in her mind. How his mouth had taken possession of hers and how he'd run his hands over her body. She'd been trembling and out of breath. And so had he.

Why couldn't she have felt that with Neil? Or any other guy she'd met?

But it had always been Mitch. Ever since the night he'd come to her after catching his wife in bed with that senator's son. Before that, if Alex were honest. But she tried so hard to keep whatever she felt strictly platonic.

Last Saturday was the closest he'd come to talking about his childhood since the night his marriage ended, and she'd blown it by pushing too hard. She'd ruined everything the past two weeks by insisting Mitch see her as a woman. And what had that gained her? Nothing but heartache. Her plan had backfired.

She'd lost her best friend.

Rubbing her eyes against a roaring headache, she trudged to her bathroom and filled her tub with hot water and vanilla-lavender bath oils. She lit some candles, stripped out of her bathing suit and sank into the bath. She needed to calm her tension headache and think about what to do. Or not think at all.

It seemed as if she'd been dealing with her feelings for Mitch half her life. She'd tried being a good friend, waiting him out, trying to get over him and, finally, moving away. Nothing had worked.

She'd thought after the way he kissed her last week that maybe… But if Mitch wanted more than friendship from her, she didn't want it to be just because he was horny. She couldn't waste anymore of her life waiting to find out if they could ever be more.

Resting her head against the rim of the tub, she closed her eyes. Suddenly her grandfather's words came back to her. *"Lexie, girl, you got to go after life like you rope a runaway calf, before it gets away."* He'd whispered it as he hugged her goodbye the day she left for the Air Force Academy. He'd been her lone supporter amidst her parents' disapproval, so at the time, she'd thought he meant her career. But now she could see how that bit of wisdom applied to the rest of her life, as well.

She sat up, sloshing water over the edge of the tub. *You know what you have to do, Hughes.*

Go after that runaway calf.

There was never going to be a good time to tell him how she felt. It was always going to be risky. For years, she'd been afraid of losing him if she told him. That he might be appalled, and things would get awkward between them. That the friendship would be ruined.

But, it seemed like that was where the relationship

was right now. Avoiding each other. Feeling awkward. What did she have to lose? What was she waiting for?

Shaking with urgency and nerves, she dried off, got dressed and hopped in her Mustang. She fought Saturday night traffic, all the while second-guessing her decision.

What if he laughed at her? Or worse, what if he let her down gently and pitied her?

Maybe he wouldn't be home. After all, it was eleven o'clock on a Saturday night. But Mitch was still honoring his thirty days of celibacy. And besides, she knew all the places he'd hang out anyway. She could find him if she had to.

Turned out there was no need. His Jeep was parked out front of his apartment. Forcing her hands to unclench from the steering wheel, Alex got out and wiped her sweaty palms on her jeans. *You can do this, Hughes.*

The closer she got to his door, the more shallow her breathing became. She couldn't draw in air. This could put the last nail in the coffin of their friendship. Turning around, she headed for her car. She was such a wimp.

No. She stopped so fast her sneakers squeaked. It was either this or live in limbo-land forever.

Drawing in a long, deep breath, she spun on her heel, marched up to his door and knocked. After the longest minute of her life, the door swung open.

Mitch was in a pair of low-riding jeans and nothing more. His chiseled chest made her pulse race. She got caught in the contours of muscles and flat brown nipples, and light dusting of blond hair, and couldn't look anywhere else. How sad was that?

"Hughes?"

The odor of liquor wafted from his breath and she finally met his gaze. His eyes were bloodshot, his hair rumpled.

Oh, Mitch. What are you doing to yourself? If only she could help him see that life could be so wonderful. He wanted love? It was standing right in front of him. She drew in a deep breath and opened her mouth… Her gaze shifted to the football game on his 55-inch flat-screen television. "Who's winning?" She pushed past him and stood behind his brown leather sofa.

Mitch shut the door, but didn't move into the room. "Tennessee. Seven to six."

"Which quarter?" Maybe she'd just watch the game first before getting into anything serious. She went to the fridge, helped herself to a beer and took a seat on his couch the way she'd done hundreds of times before.

Mitch rubbed the back of his neck. "What are you doing here, Hughes?"

Alex froze, the beer halfway to her lips. He'd never questioned her presence in his place before. Never spoken to her in such a defensive tone.

She leaned forward and placed the bottle on the coffee table. He was right. They couldn't pretend everything was okay. Couldn't go back to the way things were before.

"I wanted—" *She bit her lip. Just say it, Hughes. Tell*

him you love him. What's the worst that can happen? It took all her courage to stand and face him. The words were on the tip of her tongue as she looked up into his baby-blue eyes. What she saw there shut her down. Impatience. Irritation. And a quick glance down the hall.

So, not only did their last kiss not inspire any deeper feelings for her, but her transformation had been too much for him. He either resented her for the prank, or resented her for becoming a woman in his eyes. Her vision became jittery, her face flamed in humiliation.

"Never mind." She bolted for the door. When he didn't try to stop her, she paused with her hand on the doorknob and looked back at him.

His gaze met hers but not before she noticed he'd been staring down the hall at his bedroom door. Which—she checked—was shut. Oh. My. God. She strode down to his bedroom.

"Alex, wait." He grabbed her arm, but she wrenched it away and opened his door.

There, in the middle of the room stood a tall, voluptuous blonde in a sequined, strapless showgirl costume.

Alex glared daggers at Mitch. "But you're supposed to be—"

Mitch grimaced.

"You bastard!" Alex shoved her palms into his chest and knocked him back against the wall.

"Hughes, it's not what you th—"

"Tell it to someone who cares, *Casanova.*" Alex

marched back to the front door, but Mitch shot ahead of her and blocked her path.

She grabbed his shoulders and tried to shove him out of the way.

"Maybe I should go, hon." Alex spun to see the blonde clomping toward them in platform shoes. A long feather tail from the back of the costume swished behind her.

Alex turned back to glare at Mitch.

"It's all right, Svetlana," Mitch answered, his gaze darting behind Alex and then settling again on her.

"McCabe." Alex spoke between gritted teeth, her temper barely in check. "Get out of my way and let me out of this door before I break your gorgeous face." She reached for the doorknob.

He grabbed her wrist and had the audacity to grin. "You think my face is gorgeous?"

That was it. She couldn't take anymore. Twisting out of his hold, she doubled up her fist and swung, aiming for his nose.

The blonde screeched.

Mitch caught Alex's fist before it made contact. His grin was gone.

Fury ramped up. Years of frustration obliterated common sense. Alex swung her left.

Mitch caught that, too, and wrestled her arms behind her back.

With a grunt, she stomped on his instep.

But he knew all her moves and jerked his foot out of the way. "Hughes, calm down and let's talk about this."

But she was beyond reason; rage burned like bile in her core. "Screw you!" She struggled to get out of his hold and brought her knee up, right where it would hurt the most.

Mitch turned his hips at the last second and she hit his pelvic bone. "Goddamn it, Hughes!" He let go of her wrists, bent and caught her around her thighs, and hauled her up and over his shoulder.

Before Alex could fight free, he swatted her hard on her behind and threw her down onto his sofa. He landed hard on top of her and held her down, grabbing her hands and twining her fingers between his before forcing them up over her head.

"I think I'll wait outside, hon. Thank you for everything." Alex heard the front door click as the blonde shut it behind her.

SITUATION REPORT—DAY TWENTY-ONE: crazy as hell.

Mitch stared down at Hughes—Alex. He couldn't believe she was here. Her chest rose and fell fast with harsh breathing. Her short, silky hair was wild, flying in her eyes and catching on her damp temples. Not a bit of makeup on. And he thought she'd never looked more beautiful. As he watched, her whiskey-colored eyes sparked with fury.

"Mitch, I swear if you don't get off me right now—" She arched up, trying to shove him off.

"Alex! Calm down and listen!" He shook her and she stilled. "Svetlana is my neighbor. That's all she is, just a neighbor. She locked herself out and we were just waiting on the building manager to bring a locksmith."

Alex narrowed her eyes. "And you just happen to be laundering the shirt off your back while she was here?"

Mitch glanced down at his bare chest and shrugged. "What can I say? I wasn't dressed when she rang my doorbell."

She studied him a second longer. "If everything is so innocent, why hide her in your bedroom?"

He scoffed. "You have to ask me that after the way you reacted just now?"

She pursed her lips and let out a hard sigh. "Well, crap."

"Too bad you didn't let me explain before you almost broke my nose." He grinned.

"Yeah, that's not all I almost broke." She smirked.

"Nah. I saw that move coming a mile away. I know you too well."

The smirk faded from her sweet mouth. "Yeah. You do."

Her voice had gone all soft and her words hit Mitch somewhere in his chest.

He became aware of Alex's soft body lying beneath his, chest to chest, hip to hip, her legs notched between his. He wanted to kiss those bare lips. He wanted to bury himself inside her and stay until Christmas. This was Hughes he was thinking about. Which was nuts.

But telling himself that didn't change the fact that he wanted her.

But he'd given his word to Jackson. Man, it would chafe his pride to have to admit he'd failed. Not to mention having to pay a forfeit not of his choice. And the last time they'd kissed Alex said they couldn't be friends anymore. And he couldn't lose her friendship.

So, he'd stayed away this week. Giving her space, and him time to figure out what the hell to do. Not that he'd figured anything out...

Forcing his body to stand down, he eased off her and got to his feet. Then moved to the other side of the room, crossed his arms and leaned against his TV cabinet. "So, what did you come here for?"

She sat up and propped her elbows on her knees, studying her hands. "You didn't show up for my pool party today." A long pause. "And—we've been friends for twelve years." She took another long pause before bringing her gaze up to meet his. "I'm thirty years old, Mitch, and it's time I take the bull by the horns and—"

"Don't tell me you're marrying that squid you were dating in D.C."

She straightened. "Would it bother you if I did?"

Hell, yeah.

He made himself shrug. "I guess not. Not as long as you're happy."

She glared daggers at him.

"What?" Wasn't that how friends acted?

"Fine." She got to her feet and stuck her hands in her back pockets. "We're getting married next week."

"The hell you are!" He pushed off the cabinet and descended on her. "You barely know the guy. I haven't even met him— What are you grinning about?"

She held her ground, refusing to retreat. "Thought you said as long as I was happy…?"

"That was in the abstract." He took a couple steps closer until they were nose to nose. "This is for real." Her lips were a pale pink and as he stared at them, he couldn't think why he shouldn't kiss them.

"It is?" She swallowed, bringing attention to her delicate throat.

"Is what?" He met her gaze and caught the desire in her eyes. She wanted him, too. Damn it, why did things have to be so complicated between them?

"You're not really marrying that jerk, are you?"

She shook her head. "No."

He lowered his head and covered her mouth. She whimpered and opened for him, inviting him in. And he went willingly, probing the hot recesses of her mouth with his tongue until she moaned.

Her fingers tangled in his hair and held him tight, taking possession of the kiss with wild abandon. Her tongue seemed as determined as his to explore.

His hands wanted to explore, too. He slipped them beneath her T-shirt and ran them over her smooth skin, tracing her spine and then digging under the waistband of her jeans. His palm felt nothing but the soft flesh of her bottom.

Sweet mercy, she was wearing a thong. His pulse jumped and his cock hardened. With a moan, he squeezed her naked cheek and pushed his erection into her stomach.

He had to see Alex in only her underwear. Now. "Alex," he whispered as he kissed down her jaw to her neck. "Help me." He was frantically trying to unbutton and unzip her jeans.

As she took over he grabbed the hem of her T-shirt and slid it up over her bra. Aw, jeez, it was a purple lacy thing. He mouthed the plump mounds above her bra line, eliciting a gasp from Alex as she wiggled her jeans down her legs and kicked her shoes off.

Slowly, he let his gaze wander down her body to the purple little triangle covering her obviously shaved pussy. And there it was. The tattoo she'd told him she had. Just above the line of her thong on her left side, a tiny navy-and-silver Air Force insignia. He grinned. Only Hughes.

Inhaling her musky scent, he rubbed his fingers over the fabric, delving between her folds and circling her clit. The material was soaked through. He closed his eyes to get himself under control before he reverted to Neanderthal tactics. "Alex," he murmured. She made soft mewling noises and pushed her hips forward.

He had to taste her.

Peeling the thong down her thighs and off, he

dropped to one knee and licked and nibbled where his fingers had been.

Alex called out his name and the names of several higher powers as she grasped the back of his head. She was so responsive, so feminine. He'd never have thought...

With a secret smile, he went back to playing with her, licking and mouthing deeper between her thighs. If there was one thing he could do for a woman it was bring her pleasure. He stroked with his tongue and brought his fingers to delve inside, teasing her, rubbing and circling her swollen nub until she stiffened beneath him and cried out his name.

Her hands dropped from his head and Mitch watched as she went limp. She sighed as her breathing returned to normal.

Condom. He needed a condom. He'd removed the ones from his wallet for the duration. "Uh, I'll be right back." He shot up and made it to his bathroom medicine cabinet and back to Alex in record time.

But she was stepping into her jeans. She met his gaze and her expression wasn't encouraging. Though her eyes were still glazed with passion, her brows were creased in a frown and the soft lines of her mouth crumpled.

Sliding an arm around her waist, he gently combed the hair away from her beautiful face. "Hey." He bent to press gentle kisses across her freckled nose, her forehead, her chin and down her throat. "Don't overthink this, okay?"

"No, Mitch." She shrugged out of his grasp and zipped her jeans. "What about your thirty days? You gave your word to Jackson."

He shivered. His body screamed for release. "But I want you, Alex." After years of one-night stands, of dealing with women who wanted more than he could give or wanted to play games. Or they wanted the fantasy. The guy in the uniform. The hero fighter pilot. He was so goddamn tired of coming home bored, or worse, depressed.

Hughes wasn't like that. She knew him better than anyone, and here she was, letting him kiss his way along her neck. He couldn't believe she wanted him. Just Mitch.

She shook her head. "The minute it's over, you'll regret breaking your word. I know you, Mitch."

He sighed and closed his eyes.

"I'm sorry, Mitch. So sorry." She started gathering up her shoes.

"No, you're right." He shuddered and went to get a shirt for himself. When he returned to his living room, Alex was hunkered down tying her shoes.

She straightened and met his gaze. "I'm sorry. I shouldn't have come over here." Spinning, she headed for the door.

For the second time that night he flattened his palm on the door to prevent her leaving. "Why did you?"

She wouldn't look at him. And she was trembling. "Honest answer, Mitch." Keeping her grip on the doorknob and her gaze on his hand. "If I'd been dating the guy for over a year, and you met him and liked him, then would you be happy for me to marry him?"

Nausea rose in his stomach. She was serious. After what they'd just shared? But she'd obviously been thinking about this. The guy must've proposed. And she wanted Mitch's blessing.

Then all the pieces finally clicked into place. The way she'd been acting when she first got here. She'd come over here to tell him something. Pressure built up in his chest. She was getting married. And things would never be the same. He'd lose his best friend. This D.C. SEAL sure as hell wouldn't appreciate his wife hanging out at the officers' club drinking beer and playing pool with the guys. With Mitch.

But she was his best friend. And she thought marrying this guy would make her happy. How could he not want that?

"I guess, if he makes you happy, Hughes. Then, yeah, I wish you all the best." He almost choked on the words. But he meant them. He wanted her happiness. So, he made himself smile. "Even though I'd lose my wingman."

She didn't return his smile as he'd expected. "I don't want to lose you either, Mitch," she whispered, then yanked open the door and raced away.

He swallowed, something feeling not quite right. If

she was serious about marrying this guy, then what had tonight been to her? Getting it out of her system before she tied the knot? A quick check to see who was better? Fury shot through him. He'd never understand women.

9

SITUATION REPORT—DAY TWENTY-FOUR: pathetic.

"What the hell are you doing out here, McCabe?" Lieutenant Colonel Grady appeared at Mitch's Jeep's window.

Good question. What *was* he doing parked on the training airfield at this time of night? Morning, really. Alex was just returning from a sortie. He'd seen her Falcon land minutes ago. Even from this distance he'd recognize that Texas-shaped Texas flag she'd painted on the aircraft's nose.

Mitch faced his superior, and his friend. "Just watching the new trainees practicing their night maneuvers, sir." Yeah, right.

Grady's gaze darted to the bottle of Jim Beam in Mitch's passenger seat. "Have you been drinking?"

McCabe glanced at the bottle and then back at Grady. "Not yet."

When he'd picked up the booze earlier, he'd planned

to go home and drink until he could sleep. But he'd ended up here instead.

His insomnia hadn't improved any since Alex left Saturday night. In fact, it'd gotten worse. Couldn't concentrate. Couldn't make himself care about much. He knew Grady had been covering for him with his commander, and if he didn't get his act together, he'd earn himself a reprimand. Maybe even mess up his promotion.

"You shouldn't be out here, McCabe. Go home."

Staring out at the row of F-16s where Hughes was just coming from, McCabe ran a hand down his jaw. "Yeah. I'm going." She had a special walk. It wasn't at all masculine, but it wasn't all mincing and prancing either. It was just…Alex.

Was this SEAL guy going to appreciate that? Or any of the other special things about Hughes? Once they'd been married a few years—if it lasted that long—he'd probably find fault with her and start an affair. Hughes would be devastated.

And he couldn't stand to watch that happen.

"Look." Grady propped his fists on his hips. "I'm sure not the one to be giving advice, but…just talk to her."

Mitch winced but still kept his eye on Hughes. "I don't think she'd listen." Had he listened when Hughes tried to tell him not to marry Luanne? Of course not. That's what love did. It made a perfectly sensible person turn into a moron.

"Well, what about…" Grady shifted weight from one boot to the other. Even Mitch knew the guy was completely out of his element here. "Hey, remember when Jackson was trying to get Jordan? He sent her all those presents like flowers and a car."

Mitch gave him his full attention. "I'm not trying to 'get' her. I just don't want to lose my friend."

Grady raised one disbelieving brow.

"Besides," Mitch continued. "Can you see Hughes caring about any of that?"

"No." Grady scratched his head. "You could always fall back on the tried and true."

Mitch gave him a weary smile. "What's that?"

"Apologize."

Mitch tried to laugh but it came out sounding more like a grunt. He squeezed the bridge of his nose. "If only that was all it took." He reached out and started the Jeep's engine. "Hey, this never happened, right?"

"I don't know what you're talking about," Grady called over his shoulder as Mitch drove off.

ALEX DIDN'T REMEMBER driving home the night after leaving Mitch's house. Things were slightly blurry. The whole next day was a blur, too.

Thankfully, she had classes to teach. Air-to-air combat demanded one hundred percent of one's concentration. *The Mistake,* as she'd begun thinking of her actions Saturday night, was shoved down into the dark recesses of her brain. For eight hours each night—or most of them—she didn't give Mitch, or *The Mistake,* or her miserable love life one thought.

By the end of the week, working nights and not seeing Mitch at all, she still hadn't figured out how to undo all the damage *The Mistake* had caused. Not only had she *not* roped her calf, she'd actually let the stallion out of the corral and—oh, hell. She'd screwed up big-time. Now everything was such a mess she had no idea how to fix it.

"Captain Hughes?" Lieutenant Davis's voice snapped her out of her miserable thoughts.

"Yes, sorry." Alex blinked and her PowerPoint presentation came back into focus. She stood at the front of the classroom pointing to the screen behind her. Similar to a football game play, the drawing had arced arrows dissecting two roughly drawn aircraft. "Tonight we'll be practicing the High Yoyo."

Thank goodness this was her last class of the week.

"Half of you will fly defensive maneuvers, the other half will be attacking. Now, who wants to tell me about a High Yoyo?"

Davis—or Rooster, as he'd been named, something to do with being cocky, Alex surmised—raised his hand.

She nodded at him. "Go ahead, Lieutenant Davis."

Drew Davis was slouched in his chair, rolling a pencil between his fingers. His eyes smoldered into Alex. Ever since that night at the officers' club when he'd seen her in the red dress and come on to her, there'd been a sexual undercurrent in his attitude. "The High Yoyo is a defensive maneuver where the pilot rolls out, takes the vertical plane, pulls back on his stick until inverted, and then continues to pull on his stick until he's horizontal." Somehow, he managed to make the entire description sound like a sex act. Cocky, so cocky.

"Correct. But remember. You can't see the bandit in the dark. Night vision technology helps, but you can't always rely on computers. Before you finish this course, we'll practice all basic fighting maneuvers without night vision equipment."

Several pilot trainees had quick questions, which Alex answered, then she assigned each student to defender and attacker positions and they hit the airfield. "During this training sortie, your missiles will not be live," Alex called out to her class as she strode across the tarmac. "But you will employ evasive maneuvers and deploy your chaff and flares. How close can a missile get before you deploy chaff and flares, Davis?" She'd yet to catch him without a correct answer, but she would eventually.

"Two miles, Captain."

She nodded, foiled again.

Assigning two students to fly first, she tugged on her helmet and headed for her own F-16.

"Captain, permission to speak freely, sir." Davis had followed her.

"Go ahead, Davis." Alex halted to face the rookie.

"Have dinner with me tomorrow night."

Alex blinked. "You know squadron mates aren't allowed to fraternize, Lieutenant."

"So, if we were allowed, or I was to get assigned to a different squadron, you'd go out with me?"

"No offense, Lieutenant, but you're too young for me."

Davis stepped into her personal space, forcing her to lift her chin and look up at him. "Have you ever had a younger man, Alexandria?"

Crud. She really didn't need this. "Lieutenant, you're one more word away from getting reprimanded for insubordination. Step away and return to your squadron."

"Yes, sir." Davis saluted perfectly, spun on his heel and marched back to the other trainees waiting to fly.

She might have to do something about him sooner or later.

The rest of the night flew by, literally, teaching combat maneuvers. Not the first time she'd been thankful for her career.

The one thing in her life she hadn't wrecked yet.

The sun was just coming up Friday morning as Alex slipped her head under the water in her tub and stayed there as long as she could hold her breath. Her body remembered every touch, every kiss, every place where Mitch had devoted his exquisite expertise. Alex cupped her breasts and pressed her palms against her tightening nipples.

She lifted her face out of the water, gasping for a breath. Crud, she'd done it again. The tingling along her skin, the ache between her thighs, just the memory of Mitch's talented mouth gave her body instant recall. If she hadn't let him do that, she wouldn't have to forever live with the memory of what she'd never experience again. Ignorance, in this case, would, indeed, have been bliss.

With a sigh, she stepped out, wrapping a towel around her body, and tiptoed into the kitchen to see what she could scrounge up for dinner. Or breakfast, whichever. Working nights had her stomach confused. She opened the fridge and stood there taking stock of the contents as if she didn't already know what was there.

She jumped as she heard a car pull into her driveway and the door slam. The kitchen clock read six forty-five. Who would be here at this time of day? She waited, but no one rang the doorbell or knocked.

There'd been a string of burglaries in the neighborhood the past month. If she remembered correctly, they'd all taken place in the early morning after folks went to work. Just like now. And her firearm was locked in its safety box in the closet. Alex grabbed the largest knife from her drawer and crept toward the front window.

Slowly, she pulled back the curtain and peeked out. What the... Mitch?

He looked like Mitch, and yet he didn't. Instead of his usual nonchalant stance, he stood ramrod straight on her front porch, glaring at the front door with his fists clenched at his sides. The Mitch she knew was always impeccably dressed, in uniform or out. This morning Mitch looked haggard, unshaved, his T-shirt was stained and wrinkled, and…he was barefoot?

She turned and set the knife on her sofa table and when she peeked around the curtains again his gaze locked with hers. His eyes burned with need. She shivered as a frisson of lust shot through her.

His gaze dropped to her body and his eyes widened.

Whoa. She was still wrapped in the bath towel. Uselessly, she crossed an arm over her chest and stepped back.

He pounded on the door. "Alex."

She froze, unable to move. She shouldn't let him in. The way he was looking at her. And the way she was feeling right now. She wasn't naive. She knew where things would probably go. And if they did make love?

If she opened that door, she had a feeling things would never be the same. Not only would he be breaking his word to Jackson, but their friendship would be irrevocably changed.

And yet, wasn't it already? They weren't speaking. There was an unwanted tension between them.

"Alex?" He pounded on the door again.

Jeez, he was going to disturb her neighbors. And was she really going to leave him standing there on her doorstep? She could never do that to Mitch. Their relationship was changing, and she was mostly to blame. She'd deal, one way or the other.

Padding to the door, she reached up, clicked open the dead bolt and swung open the door.

Before she could step back, he swept inside, slammed the door behind him, and grabbed her shoulders. "Alex, don't do it."

The heat from his hands spread from her arms and set her body ablaze. His musky, masculine scent caught her offguard again. She had to think about what he'd said. "What? Don't do what?"

His eyes narrowed, and then sharpened with determination. "Don't marry that guy."

Ah. So that was it. "Oh. About that—"

"Alex, I—I need you." He swept her into his arms and kissed her, pulling her towel off at the same time. With a moan Alex curled her arms around his neck and kissed him back. "I tried staying away," he rasped.

"You did?" Heat blazed where his lips touched her sensitive skin.

He nodded. "I couldn't stop thinking about you." He pulled back and framed her face with callused hands. "I keep picturing you with him and it kills me. You belong with *me,* Alex." He grasped her bottom, lifting her, and she wrapped her legs around his waist. His kiss grew more desperate and deep as he carried her into her bedroom.

Placing her on the bed, he yanked his T-shirt off, shucked his jeans and underwear, and followed her down. With a sigh of relief he pressed his body to hers and took her mouth again.

"Alex," he mumbled against her lips. "I don't want to lose you." One hand palmed her breast and thumbed her nipple as he trailed openmouthed kisses down her jaw to her neck. He inhaled. "You smell so good. How did I never notice before that you could smell so good?"

More desperate kisses back up to her mouth where he plundered and played with her tongue. He moaned and pushed his thick erection into her thigh. "How can you marry that guy after what we…?" He nibbled down the other side of her neck. "What I…?" He lowered his head to suckle on her nipple.

She gasped and dug her fingers into his hair as pleasure-pain shot straight to her core.

"Say you want me as badly as I want you." He switched to the other nipple.

"I do want you." She lifted her head and kissed his forehead, his temple. "Mitch." How she wanted him. Had always wanted him. How many times had she caught herself yearning to pull him close and hold him? How many years had she longed for him to *see* her? To want her?

"So soft, so sweet," he murmured as his mouth moved down to her tummy and his hands gripped her hips. His tongue played with her navel, slowly inching his way between her thighs. But he stopped and raised his head to scorch her with his gaze. "How could I not have seen how beautiful you are?" His warm breath drifted to her quivering stomach.

Instead of answering, she reached to comb proprietary

fingers through his short blond hair. *You're mine now,* she was trying to tell him. *Mine to touch. Mine to protect. Mine to love.*

Closing his eyes, he turned his mouth into her palm and placed a kiss there. Then he resumed delving deep into her damp heat.

Relentless with his lips and tongue, he carried her just to the edge of ecstasy, and then pulled back on the throttle, making her whimper and beg, until finally he punched the afterburner and she soared above the stratosphere.

She was a quivering mess, barely noticing his absence to roll on protection while she drifted back to earth. Still catching her breath when he crawled back up to her.

Resting his weight on his elbows he cupped her face in his hands and kissed her gently until she could take a deep breath.

"Alex, open your eyes. Look at me."

She did. He wasn't smiling. His jaw was tight. He grasped the back of one knee and hitched her leg up over his shoulder, then plunged inside her with a hard thrust. She cried out and in that instant she'd lifted off and was ready to fly again. He moved in her with strong deep strokes.

She wiggled her hips to encourage him, faster, almost, almost… His eyes darkened as he accelerated and watched her lose it. She must have cried out and her nails dug into his shoulders as she came a second time, just as hard, and just as long. Staring into his eyes and knowing he watched her as she came made something fuse inside her and she felt a tear slide down her temple at the intense emotions.

He closed his eyes and thrust a few more times until he stilled and shuddered, groaning into her shoulder. Gradually his body relaxed. He lowered himself beside her and nuzzled under her jaw.

Alex ran her hands over his back as he snuggled closer. At last. She'd made love with Mitch. It seemed like all their lives had been building to this point. And yet, at the same time, it felt as if this was last thing that would ever have happened between them.

She should say something, but she couldn't think what. He'd broken his word to Jackson. For her? Because he thought she was going to get married? Did this mean he loved her? He hadn't said the words.

Her heart cried for the confident woman she used to be, and for the loving husband Mitch used to be. Maybe if she'd spoken up before he met Luanne…

No. What-ifs were for fools. She had to deal with the way her life was right now. What would he do if she told him she loved him right now?

With a sigh, Mitch untangled himself, sat up and headed for her bathroom. She heard the shower turn on and realized he had to be on base in less than an hour.

She rose, pulled on a shirt and panties, and went to the kitchen to make coffee. He'd have to go by his place for his uniform.

In a few minutes he appeared, dressed once again.

Having no idea what to say, she poured them both a mug of coffee. "You want some toast?"

He shook his head. "Nah, thanks." He sipped his coffee.

She moved to put away the bread.

"Alex." He touched her hand, then smoothed a lock of her hair off her face. "You can't marry that guy now," he said. "Not after this."

A hard lump formed in her throat. She nodded. "Get to work. We'll talk later."

After he left, she crawled back in bed, pulled her knees up, and lay there breathing in the lingering scent of Mitch.

10

SITUATION REPORT—DAY TWENTY-SEVEN: best damn day of his life.

It occurred to Mitch as he was leaving his office Friday evening that he didn't need to count down the thirty days of his celibacy anymore since that ship had sailed this morning.

Guilt at breaking his word rubbed his conscience raw. The one thing he never thought he'd do was break his word. He owed Jackson a forfeit. For three damn days. If only he could've waited three more days.

But the thought of Alex marrying that SEAL had torn up his insides. He'd meant to just go over there and talk some sense into her. To tell her marriage was for suckers. For poor saps like he used to be who bought into the whole happily ever after scam. When vows meant next to nothing these days, and love was obliterated at the first sign of hardship.

But seeing Alex in nothing but that towel had wiped

his brain clean like a computer virus on a motherboard. The next thing he knew they were both naked on her bed.

Mitch grinned as he fired up his Jeep and headed for Hughes's—Alex's—house. Who'd have thought he'd be attracted to his best friend? This would be the best of both worlds. His wingman. And his lover.

At the last minute, he stopped for Kung Pao Chicken. Alex loved Kung Pao. He couldn't ever remember feeling so…happy. So sure about anything. Even his wedding day he'd been nervous despite telling Hughes that his love felt right. He remembered feeling as if he needed to puke as he'd stood at the front of that church waiting for Luanne to walk down the aisle.

Maybe he should've paid more attention to his gut.

But his gut was just fine and dandy tonight. He hadn't had such great sex in he didn't know when. Sex had been pretty meaningless for a long time now. But with Alex…

Hard to explain why. Maybe it was a trust thing. She knew him like no one else. And he knew without a doubt he could always rely on Alex. That was real. So the sex felt more real.

As he pulled into her driveway, that thought triggered another. He'd always be there for Alex, too. Like good friends, they cared about each other. He sure felt better when he was around her. The past week had been pure hell thinking he'd lose her friendship when she married.

He got out and rang her doorbell. Maybe she'd be

wrapped in nothing but a towel again. This morning her skin had been glistening from her bath and her hair, still damp, had clung to her cheek. He'd wanted to crash through that window and hold her, taste her, have her.

Hmm, she wasn't answering. She wasn't home? Hadn't she known he'd come over here tonight? Guess he hadn't actually made plans. He'd just assumed. *Yeah, and you know what happens when you assume, Mc-Cabe.*

He turned back to his Jeep, that bad feeling forming in his gut. He'd thought they'd finally worked out their problems. Wait. She'd said they'd talk later.

Just as he opened the door to his Jeep, her Mustang pulled into her driveway. He headed her way and saw pots of shrubs, flats of multicolored flowers and huge bags of soil filling her backseat.

"Oh, hey, you're here." Alex barely glanced at him as she got out and reached into the backseat for a plant. "Help me carry this stuff to the back?"

All day he'd been thinking of being with her and she'd been thinking about yard work? He held up his bag of food. "I brought dinner."

"Great." She gave him the halfhearted smile he'd seen her use for fools and morons. "Let's get this unloaded and then we'll eat."

Did she not want him here? Should he go? With a mental shrug, Mitch stuck the bag of Kung Pao between his teeth, shrugged out of his uniform coat and set them both on the porch swing. Then he grabbed both bags of soil, hefted them onto his shoulders and carried them through the gate to the back.

After dropping the soil where Alex instructed him, he made two more trips to the car. She'd seemed surprised to see him—or had that been disappointment? Had she planned on unloading all these plants and stuff herself?

"There's a game on, want to eat on the sofa and watch?" she called as she set down the last of the flowers.

"Absolutely."

After they'd cleaned up and retrieved the Kung Pao, he grabbed a couple of beers from the fridge, loosened his uniform tie and slid it off.

She plopped down, propped her feet on the coffee table and grabbed the remote.

An hour later, Mitch thought he might be in heaven. They were still on the couch, still watching the game, but after he'd finished eating, he'd scooted closer and put his arm around Alex's shoulders. He was playing with her hair and thinking about all the things he wanted to do to her tonight.

He was glad they'd finally done what they'd done this morning. She wanted him as much as he wanted her. Just thinking that, feeling it, made him smile so big he probably looked like a dope.

She seemed completely absorbed in the game, and he didn't know why he wasn't, the score was close and the time left was short, but all he cared about right now was getting Alex beneath him. He'd been rock-hard for half an hour.

Like a teen on a first date, he was nervous, wondering how the night would play out. "So, we're good?"

She looked over at him. Her eyes seemed to be searching for something in his. Then she shrugged. "I can't fight it anymore. We'll just see where this goes, okay?"

A sense of relief overwhelmed him and he knew he was grinning like an idiot again. Surely it wasn't good that he cared that much. But this was Alex. She'd never screw him over.

Just before she turned her attention back to the game, she smiled at him and it took his breath away. He had to close his eyes and force air into his lungs. Alex's smile was one of his favorite things about her. She wasn't classically beautiful, she had more of a girl-next-door kind of prettiness. But when she smiled at him just now, he felt it to his toes.

After a second's hesitation, he wrapped his arms around her and pulled her tighter. "Alex." He nuzzled into her neck. "Do you really want to finish watching the game?"

"Mitch." She sighed as she put her cheek on his chest. "What am I going to do with you?"

"I have a few ideas." He scooped her up onto his lap. One hand lifted her T-shirt while the other traveled down beneath her sweats to play between her thighs.

"Open for me," he whispered as he tossed her shirt aside and unhooked her bra one-handed.

With a whimper she complied, spreading her legs. Supporting her with his other arm around her back, he slid a finger deep inside her, stroked her G-spot, pulled out and plunged back in. She made a strangled sound and wiggled her hips.

"Aw, Alex. You're so beautiful. Now lift your breast to me." When she cupped her breast, he lowered his head and took the tiny, pale pink nipple into his mouth and suckled, all the while thrusting with his finger, and letting his thumb tease her clit.

She arched her back and rolled her other nipple between her thumb and finger, but Mitch wanted it. He lifted her toward him and suckled it deep into his mouth, then took it gently between his teeth and flicked his tongue across the tight peak.

Crooning an incoherent sound, she sat up, slid her sweats and panties down and off, and then straddled his lap. She unbuttoned his shirt, then reached for his slacks, unzipped him and took out his hard, aching cock.

"Wait, wait." He scrambled for the condom in his back pocket and ripped it open, but she was stroking him and bent to lick the tip. Mitch lifted his hips and groaned. "Careful." He jerked when she licked him again and took him farther into her mouth and sucked. "Alex."

She looked up and met his gaze with a wicked grin.

"You're evil." With an answering grin he rolled on protection, grabbed her waist and lifted her into position. She put her hands on his shoulders and sank slowly around him.

So tight. So hot. Mitch squeezed his eyes shut and concentrated on lasting. But when she rose up on her knees and sank back down he knew it was a losing battle. "Alex, hold still," he warned through clenched teeth.

She ignored him and moved faster, fighting his hold around her waist. Up and down, she rose and fell, like everything she did, single-mindedly, skillfully, generously.

So much for lasting. He threw back his head and cursed under his breath as wave after wave of intense pleasure hit him. Even after he stiffened beneath her she didn't let up, but kept pumping him, milking him into shuddering after-spasms. Finally she jerked her hips and moaned her own pleasure before collapsing against his damp chest.

He wrapped his arms around her back and held her close, his throat tight for some reason. All he could think was, this was Alex. Skin to skin. The perfect lover for him. They'd known each other so long, that, like working on their cars, or teaching air combat, they hardly needed words to get it right. And this felt so right.

After some homemade peach ice cream, Alex took his hand and led him back to the bedroom and he made slow, tender love to her, relishing every moment, worshipping every inch of her. He couldn't believe he'd spent the last half-dozen or more years just putting tab B into slot A. Sex was much more fulfilling when the two partners knew each other so well.

When he finally came, after making Alex come again and again, he looked into her eyes just before he exploded in pleasure, and something passed between them, something unspoken, but profound. He rolled to his back as he moved off her and covered his eyes with his arm. Damn, he'd almost teared up for a second there. He'd never felt so close to anyone. It made him realize how alone he'd been all his life.

Alex rolled over and threw an arm and a leg over him, snuggling close as her breathing became slower and deeper. Then he heard a light but steady snore.

He smiled. He definitely wasn't alone anymore.

ALEX WAS COCOONED in heat. She tried to move and a band of strength tightened around her lungs. Had she crashed her jet? A deep moan sounded behind her and an unmistakable hard length twitched against her butt.

Her eyes flew open when the horny man who was curled around her pushed a knee between her legs and the hand encircling her waist moved up to cup her breast.

As he rolled over and came up on his knees, he lifted her hips, spread her thighs, and slid deep inside her in one swift movement. She cried out. The position enhanced the sensations. He filled her completely, hitting her G-spot and her womb with each thrust. With one hand teasing her clit and the other her nipple, she was a goner in a matter of minutes.

He kissed her neck, her back, her neck again before calling her name. Gripping her waist with both hands, he started pumping faster until he stiffened, breathing harshly into her shoulder.

"Mmm," he mumbled as he fell to his side and tugged her close against him.

"Mmm, yourself." Totally energized, she scooted away and hopped off the bed.

Mitch rolled to his stomach and laid his head on his bent arms.

"Come on, sleepyhead, we're burning daylight." As she headed for the shower, she slapped his taut, naked butt. He merely grunted.

Then she stopped and simply took in the sight of him.

She wished she had a camera so she could always remember this gloriously naked, slim-hipped man lying in her bed. In that position his shoulder blades protruded and his biceps bulged. The sunlight gleamed off his blond hair and seemed to radiate from his smooth, tanned skin. He was a Greek god, a supermodel and a Hollywood hunk all rolled into one.

And for now, he was all hers.

She'd showered, made coffee and stuck cinnamon rolls from a can in the oven before Apollo deigned to show his blond-stubbled jaw in the kitchen. He ruffled a hand through his hair and shuffled in, wearing only his boxer-briefs. Squinting at her, he inhaled. "Smells good."

"Well, hurry up and eat. We've got a lot to get done today."

"We do?" He poured himself a mug of coffee and sat at her table.

Guess he wasn't quite the Saturday morning enthusiast she was. "Uh, hello? All those flowers aren't going to plant themselves." She stuck her hand inside an oven mitt, pulled the rolls from the oven and slathered on the icing from the tiny plastic container.

He sipped his coffee. "Right."

Alex froze. "I mean, that's what I'm doing today. You may have other plans." She sneaked a glance at him.

Slouched in his chair, his mug halfway to his mouth, Mitch was staring at her. He set down the mug, got up and stalked over to her, lithe as a jungle cat. He slid his arms around her waist and nuzzled into her neck. "Give me half an hour to bring back a change of clothes and my shaving kit, and then your wish will be my command."

Alex smiled, warmed inside where a moment ago she'd gone cold. "That's a dangerous concept."

He reached around her, snatched a cinnamon roll off the baking sheet and popped it in his mouth. "I'll bring you an apron and you can make me a pie." He swatted her behind and then darted for the hallway.

Grabbing an onion from the hanging basket, she charged after him and pitched it at his back, but he ducked, swiveled and tackled her. Half tickling her, half carrying her into the bedroom, he dropped her on the bed and kept tickling her. Laughing and giggling, she kicked and screeched, fighting off his attack.

Alex decided the best defense was a good offense so she cupped his package and caressed.

"Aw, Hughes, no fair." His light blue eyes sparkled down at her as he lowered his head and kissed her. His body followed and soon they were writhing around on the sheets. Alex rolled on top, straddled his waist and combed her fingers through his hair as she poured all her overpowering emotions into her kiss.

His hands caressed her back, and as she tucked her nose into the strong column of his neck his arms tightened around her. They lay there just holding each other. She heard his ragged breathing soft in her ear, and she felt his Adam's apple move as he swallowed. The silence filled with words unspoken, with emotions unexpressed.

It was either spill her guts, or get up. She rolled off him and the bed and landed on her feet, forcing a smile. "Daylight's a-wasting. Come on, up and at 'em."

He rose up on his elbows, a mock expression of dismay on his face. "You're just going to leave me like this?"

Alex's gaze traveled from his face down his fine chest to the long protrusion beneath his underwear. She licked her lips. So tempting. But she'd bought those flowers on purpose to remind her that her life was more

than just Mitch. If she let him, he'd engulf her in his
life and she'd very easily lose her own. And then what
would she have when this ended, as it surely would?

She had no illusions about what she'd agreed to.
She'd simply been unwilling to live the rest of her life
without knowing what it could be like with Mitch.

"You need to save your strength." She made herself
turn and head for the backyard.

The rest of the day was a snapshot of Alex's dream
of a perfect day. In between hours of backbreaking but
fulfilling work, she and Mitch played. They chased, and
wrestled, they had a water fight and made slow love
in the pool. To her, food tasted better, the sun shone
brighter, the grass was literally greener, the water bluer.
Everything in her world was enhanced by her love for
Mitch.

And as she fell asleep in his arms for the second
night in a row, she ignored the dread and fear lurking,
waiting for the dream world she'd stolen to come crum-
bling down. She shoved it way down deep and sighed
into hot masculine skin.

11

SITUATION REPORT—DAY TWENTY-NINE: amazed.

The daily Sit-Rep a habit now, Mitch paused in the act of shaving on Sunday afternoon and stared at himself in Alex's bathroom mirror. How could the face in the mirror look the same as it always did when the man inside was a stranger?

Mitch McCabe never spent the night at a woman's house. Wasn't that the point of going to her place instead of his? So he could get up and leave whenever he wanted. No mushy snuggling. No weird mornings after. No false promises to call. No messy entanglements. Those were the rules, right?

But he hadn't given any of that one damn thought all weekend. He didn't want to get up and leave. He liked lying in Alex's arms after sex. And he liked waking up with her. All these years he'd been missing out on what was now his new favorite thing: morning sex.

This morning he'd woken up sore as hell from all

that yard work—okay, he may have exaggerated his pain slightly—and Alex had reached into her bedside table drawer for a tube of lotion.

"Roll over on your stomach," she'd ordered, and he'd obeyed willingly enough.

She'd straddled his butt, squeezed some lotion into her palms and then kneaded his shoulders and the back of his neck with the perfect blend of strength and gentleness.

"Where'd you learn to give such a great massage?"

She'd paused. "You don't want to know."

He'd had a massage from Lily before. That's how he'd met her. Had some guy taught Alex? The image of Alex lying nude while some guy put his hands all over her had made him bristle with irritation. "Was it that SEAL?"

"Settle down, Casanova," she'd said as she swatted his butt. "Every cowgirl learns to give her horse a good rubdown after a hard ride." She'd bent down and sprinkled tiny kisses down his spine.

Of course that had led to his complaint that he hadn't been ridden hard yet. And Alex had obliged. And then there was the showering together after…

Oh, yeah. Mitch smiled as he resumed his shave. He could get used to this friends-with-benefits lifestyle.

There were only a few hours left before Alex would have to leave for work. He frowned at his reflection in the mirror. She was on night maneuvers for another few weeks, so it'd be a while before—

"What are you doing, shaving every hair individually?" Alex appeared in the bathroom doorway. "My grandmother could get ready faster than you." She leaned a shoulder on the door frame and crossed her arms, one corner of her mouth lifted in an indulgent smile.

Mitch returned her smile in the mirror as he wiped his jaw with a wet cloth. "This kind of perfection doesn't happen all by itself, you know."

She rolled her eyes and pushed off the frame. "We'll be sitting in a dark theater, Casanova. And speaking of which—" she pulled her cell phone off her belt clip "—we're going to be late if we don't leave right now."

He winced at the moniker he'd been given years ago. Until recently it hadn't bothered him, he'd kind of liked it. But lately he didn't, especially coming from Alex. Although he could hear the ribbing he'd get if he told her that. "Just need to throw on a shirt." Before brushing past her to head to the closet, he stopped, caught her in his arms and kissed her behind her ear. "Or we could skip the movie and go back to bed."

Her hands came up, flattened on his chest and pushed him. "I may not be able to walk afterward if we do."

Nodding, he dropped his arms from around her and went to her closet where his shirt hung. As he reached for it, he saw his uniform suit coat and slacks hanging beside it, and the cargo shorts and shirt he'd worn yesterday stuffed in her dirty clothes hamper. It felt so... domestic. Like when he'd been married.

He shoved his arms into the sleeves and started buttoning the freshly dry-cleaned shirt, remembering how he'd liked sharing a bedroom with a woman. Having her things around, mixed with his. Liked the feeling of lives joined, of a shared future. Then he thought about returning to his empty apartment tonight after Alex went to work. Alone.

"Hey, we don't have to go." Alex's hands slid around his waist from behind.

"No." He turned and hugged her. "It'll be fun to get out. We'll grab something to eat after."

The movie was an action-packed shoot 'em up—Alex's choice—and Mitch discovered she took on violent tendencies while watching that kind of movie. He tried to hold her hand, but she wasn't going for any of that sappy stuff. She kept gripping his forearm and digging her nails in, and worse, she was a popcorn-hogger.

And he loved it. It was so…Hughes. All he could do was grin, and then take her out for a burger and sit back and watch as she built herself a Dagwood with plenty of mustard and onion rings, and he didn't even want to know what all she had inside that bun.

"Want a bite?" She offered the monstrosity across the table to him.

"Uh, no. Thanks." He leaned back, hands up as if to ward off evil.

"Wimp." She shook her head and pursed her lips just before she dug in.

"I think the only professional personnel equipped to handle that thing is HAZMAT."

"Ha-ha." She chewed and swallowed. "Neil used to say I had a cast-iron stomach."

"Who's Neil?" Probably one of her brothers. He made a mental note to ask about her family's names.

"The guy I was dating in D.C."

Mitch froze with his fajita halfway to his mouth. "You're kidding, right? Neil, the SEAL?" He threw an arm across the back of the booth and hooted.

"Hey, don't laugh. He's a decorated hero."

"That may be, but the poor guy should've chosen a different branch of the military." He snickered. "Or changed his name."

Alex glared at him, but he could tell she was trying not to smile. She finally broke and chuckled. "I shouldn't laugh, he's a sweet guy."

Mitch didn't like the way her expression went all soft when she talked about him. "What'd he get a medal for?"

"Remember a few years back when those pirates captured that freighter ship off the coast of Yemen?"

He grunted.

"And the president ordered those sharpshooter SEALs to take them out?"

"And Neil-the-SEAL made the shot?" Great. His rival *was* a freakin' hero. "He must get lots of tail off that story."

"As a matter of fact, the only way I found out was through his friend. Neil doesn't talk about it."

Fantastic. A *modest,* sweet hero. "It's a wonder you didn't marry Mr. Perfect right then and there."

"I know. His father is a United States senator. His mother is on the boards of several charitable foundations. So what the heck am I doing here with you?" Her eyes widened in mock exasperation and she smirked just before she took another huge bite of her hamburger.

She was trying to laugh this off, but Mitch couldn't help but wonder, seriously, what *was* she doing here with him? His stomach cramped up. *Another freakin' senator's son?*

He hated that he'd told Alex about his background. She hadn't judged him at the time, but compared to a guy with such a distinguished family? And besides, she didn't know all the details.

He'd never forget the look in Luanne's eyes after he'd told her about the horror of his childhood, certain that she wouldn't judge him. And then seeing the disgust mixed with pity whenever she looked at him after that.

"Mitch," Alex recalled his attention back to the here and now. "You know I was just kidding, right? If I wanted to be with Neil, I would be."

He lifted a shoulder, shrugged it off. "Hell, yeah. Just think, I might have had to call you Mrs. Neil-the-SEAL."

She put a pickle on the edge of a fork and catapulted the thing across the table at him.

He ducked and it missed. "Starting a food fight, Hughes? I can't take you anywhere."

Too soon he was kissing her goodbye as she stood at the door of her house in her pressed uniform and leather briefcase ready for the base.

"Is that rookie still bothering you?" Mitch frowned. Just what he needed. More competition in the form of a younger, cockier *him*.

"Who, Davis?" She pressed her lips to Mitch's neck and spread kisses up to his jaw as she spoke. "Didn't I tell you? He's got himself a girlfriend."

"Good." Mitch wasn't sure whether to be grateful or worried about the poor guy. "I'd hate to have to beat him up."

She drew away and shook her head. "I've told you before I can take care of myself."

"Yeah, well, I've got your back, Hughes."

"Not on base. We don't want to give our commanders any more reasons to suspect we're seeing each other."

On that they agreed. "Absolutely."

"So," she said. "Will you be here in the morning?" Her hands were running over his chest and up his arms, making it hard to concentrate on her words.

Monday morning. The start of the normal workweek. The return to everyday life. "Uh, yeah, maybe." He nodded, not sure why he was hedging. But maybe they shouldn't get too comfortable. Take things for granted.

"Oh-kay? Call me, then, so I'll know whether to go on to sleep."

"You bet." He gave her a quick kiss.

She hesitated, searching his eyes, and then she was gone. Her car disappearing in the distance.

Mitch, confused, walked to his Jeep. What the hell had just happened here? He only knew their parting had been awkward. And as much as he'd hated that, he couldn't think what to do about it.

Later, Mitch rolled over, opened a bleary eye and cursed. He'd overslept. Jumping out of bed, he threw on his uniform and raced to his office, ducking in twenty minutes after eight.

As he grabbed his clipboard off his desk he realized Alex was probably already asleep. Not that he had a spare minute to pick up the phone. He jogged down several corridors to his classroom and barely made it ahead of his students. Ah, well, he'd stop by her house tonight.

What was that old adage about the best-laid plans? By five he was still working on reports he'd neglected for weeks and when he finally glanced at the clock it was after seven-thirty.

Grabbing his jacket and keys, he headed for his Jeep. Alex might already be on base—he stopped in his tracks—but, for now it'd be better for their careers if they kept their distance at work. Neither of their commanders would approve of them hooking up. Even though they were technically on different squadrons, they still flew together sometimes.

And a call right now would only disrupt her class. She'd probably be in the air most of the night anyway.

At home, he sat mindlessly in front of the television all evening, fell asleep on the couch and was late waking up the next morning, also. By the time he thought to call Alex, his reasons for not contacting her the day before didn't seem quite as legitimate, and he had no idea what he'd say, so he put it off.

Tuesday night he fell asleep thinking he probably should call her tomorrow...

WHEN MITCH DIDN'T show up or call Monday morning, Alex went on to sleep, figuring she'd hear from him that evening before she left for work. When he still hadn't called Tuesday evening, she couldn't decide whether to cry or kill him.

She'd never been a crier.

Wednesday morning she drove straight from work to Mitch's apartment, noting the spectacularly gorgeous sunrise. Purple and pink clouds outlined in sparkling golden light streaked across the lavender sky. Funny how the earth could produce such beauty when her world was a steaming pile of...thunderclouds.

Without making time to second-guess her actions, she parked in front of his place, marched up to his door and rang the bell. After a few seconds without an answer, she rang it again and then pounded on the door. It was still another few seconds before the door opened.

Wearing wrinkled shorts and a shirt, Mitch squinted

at her, his hair rumpled. He was scratching his jaw and she drew her fist back and sucker punched him right in the gut.

With a grunt he doubled over grabbing his stomach.

Ah, watching him gasp for air and seeing the look of shock on his face gave her immense satisfaction. Her chin upturned, she marched off.

"Alex, what the hell?" He squeaked out the words.

Oh, like he had no idea why she'd be so furious? She kept going. Then she heard a horrible sound and glanced behind her.

Still clutching his stomach, Mitch had dropped to his knees and was throwing up into the bushes beside his door.

Closing her eyes, she hesitated. But no. She refused to feel guilty. Hardening her heart, she continued to her car.

Just as she was starting the ignition, Mitch reached in and grabbed her hand. "Alex, wait a goddamn minute!"

She yanked her hand out of his grasp, but he got hold of her keys and was headed back to his apartment.

Her fury ramped up again and she jumped out and chased after him. "McCabe, you give those back to me!"

She tried to snatch her keys, but he held them out of her reach. "Not until you tell me what's going on."

She grabbed his arm and tried to wrestle them away from him.

"Jeez, Hughes, you ever consider an anger management class? Ow! Stop kicking. Now, settle down."

As hard as she tried, she couldn't wrestle her keys from his grasp, which infuriated her even more. "Don't make me really hurt you, you knuckle-dragging ape."

As she yelled, Mitch cast a few furtive glances around the apartment complex. "Come inside before someone calls the cops." He took her arm, but she jerked it away.

"Forget it!"

"Oh for the love of—" He took her keys, stuffed them down the front of his shorts and retreated inside his apartment.

Breathing hard, fists at her sides, she followed him in and slammed the door. Her insides churned with impotent frustration and humiliation. "You think sticking them down your underwear will stop me?"

Muttering a string of curses, he trudged into the kitchen and she heard the water running a moment before he reappeared wiping his mouth with a towel. Falling onto the sofa, he leaned his head back and closed his eyes.

Why had she come here? She'd known it wouldn't last. She'd known that once she was intimate with him she'd become just another conquest to him. She shook her head. "You know, the least you could've done was have the balls to tell me it's over to my face."

He lifted his head and pierced her with a puzzled expression. "What?"

"I am not one of your bimbo, booty call, notch-on-your-joystick nobodies that you can sleep with and then ignore and move on. Now give me my keys." She held out her hand.

He reached in and got them out, then extended them to her. "Can I explain?"

Her fury dissipated into a profound sadness. "I don't think there's anything left to say."

He dropped the keys to his side and his head onto the back of the couch again. "Jeez, that punch hurt."

Guilt stabbed at Alex but not enough to ask if he was okay. The best she could manage was to stand and wait for him to explain. She folded her arms and tapped her foot repeatedly. "Anytime before Christmas, Casanova."

Avoiding her gaze, he sat up and dropped his elbows onto his knees. "I've never been here before, Alex." He rubbed the back of his neck. "You know. It's strange." He grimaced. "I mean, it's not bad strange—but because we're best friends, I keep thinking maybe this isn't good."

Stunned, she could barely speak. "What does that mean?"

He finally looked at her. "You can do better than me. You got a hero SEAL, a senator's son after you. I can't compete with that."

"I didn't realize this was a competition."

"Let's be honest, Hughes. If you were still stationed at Langley, we both know you'd be with ol' Neil."

Alex snorted. "Shows what you know. You think I

could ever bring the guy home? I can hear it now, every freakin' Christmas my brothers would surround me in the kitchen, 'So, Alex, how the hell is Neil-the-SEAL? When are y'all gonna have a litter of spotted pups?'"

Mitch chuckled. She caught just a flash of those adorable dimples before he grabbed his stomach and winced in pain. "Ow, it hurts to laugh."

"Serves you right." But the anger was gone from her words. She shook her head. "I told you Sunday night. If I wanted to be with Neil, I would be. Don't you know me well enough by now to know I do what I want?"

His expression cleared as if he'd just figured out some quantum equation. "Yeah." He nodded. "You do, don't you?"

She heaved a big exasperated sigh. "Honestly, Mitch. What am I going to do with you?"

He stood. "Whatever you do, avoid my midsection. I have to get to the base."

"Don't you think you ought to see the doctor?"

"Nah." Closing the distance between them, he ran his knuckles down her cheek. "I'm an idiot."

"Yes, you are." Now that her anger had dissipated, the adrenaline left her shaking. Determined to get out of here before he saw her hands trembling, she snatched her keys off the sofa and headed for the door. Moving fast, he caught her by the shoulders.

Slowly, he lowered his head and lightly brushed his lips across hers. "Can I come over after work tonight?"

Alex's heart squeezed. She wanted to howl her

frustration to the world. Being with him was nothing short of emotional suicide. And despite her recent decisions, she didn't have a death wish. No. She'd tell him no and rip off the bandage all at once. "Okay."

He grinned and took her mouth in a deep possessive kiss.

Okay? She was pathetic. She shouldn't be letting him kiss her.

"I have some time before I have to be at work," he mumbled as his lips trailed down her jaw to her neck. His hand crept under her shirt and cupped her breast and his hot palm kneading her flesh drove all rational thought away. His other hand cupped her butt and lifted her, walking to his sofa. And she didn't fight him.

So, she was officially an addict, avoiding reality. Craving one more hit, one more day of Mitch. Like a drug she never should've tried in the first place. He made her weak. He made her lose all sense of reason. But she was hooked.

Was there such a thing as a Mitch McCabe rehab?

12

SITUATION REPORT: sucker punched by girlfriend. Wait…
girlfriend?

"Hey, if it isn't Monk-man McCabe!" Sanders taunted as Mitch got in line to grab a sandwich at the commissary.

Mitch gritted his teeth, smiled and nodded. Let the guy have his fun. Mitch wasn't about to risk his promotion.

"Keep up, Sanders." Grady joined the lunch line. "His thirty days were over yesterday."

"Is that so?" Sanders narrowed his eyes, a sly look on his face. "What? No Hughes around to defend you today, McCabe?"

"Why? You miss getting your ass handed to you, Sanders?"

Sanders scowled. "Heard she's on night maneuvers." He leaned in. "With Rooster in her class, I bet she's maneuvering every night."

Mitch gritted his teeth. His hands curled into fists. Then he raised his brows and snapped his fingers. "Yeah, that's right. You'd know about Hughes's maneuvering, wouldn't you? How is your foot doing, by the way?"

Sanders lost his smile. Mitch chuckled all the way back to his office. Good thing Hughes hadn't been with him. She'd have cleaned poor Sanders's clock.

A warmth grew in his chest thinking about her. About how she'd put up with Sanders's groping that night, but the minute the guy insulted Mitch, she'd lost it. Nobody had ever fought for him before. Or believed in him like she did. Even this morning, she'd been fighting for him.

When Alex wanted something, she went after it, no holds barred. And pity the fool who got in her way, which he had. Most women who didn't get called for three days would've written him off, or maybe called to whine and complain.

Even Luanne, after they'd been married a few months, he'd wake up in the middle of the night and hear her crying in the bathroom. He'd get up and ask her what was wrong, and she'd say, "Nothing."

How could you fight nothing? How could you solve the "nothing" problem?

He'd bet his flight suit he'd never have that problem with Alex. He wouldn't even have to ask. She'd come out and tell him what the problem was, and probably tell him what he could do about it, too.

He grinned just thinking about her, and as soon as he got off, he raced for her house, thinking about the incredible makeup sex they could have.

So much that he didn't notice the flashing lights behind him at first.

Crap. Of all the times to get stopped for speeding.

He pulled over and got out his license and proof of insurance. From his side mirror he saw the cop striding toward him. As the officer reached his Jeep's open side and removed his sunglasses, Mitch looked up.

"Jackson?" Mitch hadn't yet told his ex-Air Force buddy he owed him a forfeit.

"You aware you were smiling, McCabe?"

"Yeah, I kno— Smiling? You mean speeding."

"No, but—" he reached into his back pocket and pulled out his ticket book "—I can write you a ticket if—"

"No, that's okay."

"I pulled you over to inform you your thirty days are officially over. But I can see from your cocky grin you already knew that."

"Yeah, about that. I, uh. I didn't make it."

Jackson raised his brows and blinked. "Real funny, McCabe. Pull the other one."

It took every ounce of manipulation Mitch had ever learned to convince Jackson he had actually broken his word without revealing with whom or why. The only forfeit Mitch wouldn't agree to was another thirty days.

They finally settled on a full weekend of helping

Jackson and Jordan move out of their tiny apartment into a new home. They both knew Mitch would've helped anyway, but it was this weekend and they planned to treat everyone to barbecue ribs as a thank-you as soon as they finished Sunday night.

Everybody.

As Mitch drove off, waving to Jackson, it wasn't a question of whether Alex had been invited, or even if she would go. No, the question was, would he and she go together? Or keep their affair a secret?

The makeup sex before she left for work was short and sweet. He hated that they only had a couple of hours together during the week. It wasn't nearly enough time. He couldn't wait for Friday night, and spending the weekend with her. Even if they'd be moving furniture and boxes most of the time. Being with Alex would make the job fun. Never a dull moment with her.

MITCH PULLED INTO Alex's driveway Friday night and let himself in the front door. Something smelled really good and his stomach growled. He made his way into the kitchen and the first thing he saw was the table. Where she usually had her laptop, her briefcase and a dozen other odds and ends was now a clean surface set with real plates and candles.

Then he looked over and saw Alex pulling a pot roast out of the oven. The sink and counters were cluttered with bowls, all the stuff that had been on the table, and days' worth of things not put away. That was more like the Alex he knew. But the roasting pan in her hands wasn't. He blinked and shook his head.

She caught sight of him and smiled. "Oh, good. I'm glad you're home. Could you loosen the gasket on the pipe under the bathroom sink? It's leaking."

Mitch stood, frozen in bewilderment and…something else that felt funny in his gut. "I thought you said you couldn't cook?"

She took off her oven mitts, tossed them on the counter and shoved hair out of her eyes with the back of her hand. "I said I didn't want to be stuck cooking and cleaning all day. Doesn't mean I don't know how to make dinner."

Mitch didn't know what to say, so he just stood there.

"What?" Her lips had flattened.

"Nothing. Smells good. I'll get my wrench."

Before checking the pipe, he changed out of his uniform and pulled on some shorts. While he was on his back halfway under the bathroom sink, Alex appeared in the doorway. "I just replaced one of the gaskets in the other bath, so I figured that's what this was. But I could *not* get the dang thing loose."

Mitch pulled with all his might to loosen the fitting. "Got it."

"Jeez, it sucks being a female when it comes to upper body strength. No matter how hard I work out…"

Mitch scooted out and sat up. "I have to say, I'm awfully glad you're female." He smiled and wiggled his brows.

Her frown disappeared and her eyes twinkled. She hunkered down, put her hand behind his head and kissed him hard and deep. Her tongue played around his and her other hand traveled down his shoulder to his arm.

Slowly, she released his mouth, squeezed his biceps and smiled. "I have to admit. Watching you show off your guns while you tugged on that thing really turned me on."

"Oh, yeah?" Dropping the wrench, he cupped her cheek and pressed short kisses to the corners of her mouth, her nose, her eyes, her temple.

She pulled back. "I was going to wait until after dinner for this, but…" She grabbed the hem of her T-shirt and drew it up over her head and off, tossing it out to the hall.

He momentarily lost his breath when he saw her bra. It cupped and lifted her breasts, but only covered the bottom half of them in baby-blue satin.

"You like?"

He grunted and thumped his chest with the side of his fist. "Me like."

She giggled and he savored the sound. "I bought this color 'cause it matched your eyes."

"You did?" She'd thought about his eyes? The more he got to know this woman, the more she blew him away. He dragged his gaze away from her breasts and looked up into her golden-brown eyes. "Baby, you amaze me."

"Oh, Mitch." Her hands gripped his head and she straddled him right there on the floor.

With a groan he palmed her breasts and kissed the soft mounds, sliding the straps down as far as he could.

He wasn't sure who undressed who or even how they both fit in the tiny bathroom, he just closed his eyes and held on as she took his pulsing erection inside her tight warmth. He heard her ragged breathing, and his. Heard her cry of pleasure and his. Then he held her tight as she lowered her chest to his. Her flesh was soft and sweet and damp and he wanted to hold her like this forever.

The warmth that had started in his chest the other day had grown into a heat blast of emotion he could barely contain behind prickling eyes. He knew now why he'd felt so funny when he walked in tonight. She'd said, "Glad you're *home*." And he *was* home. Here. Inside her. With her.

"Mitch?"

"Yeah?"

She lifted her head and stared into his eyes. Her lips parted and then closed again. There was something in her eyes, some yearning, something she needed… "Never mind." She laid her head back on his chest.

Aw, Hughes. He squeezed his eyes closed. "Don't do that. Tell me."

Her soft breath warmed his cooling chest and he rubbed his chin on the top of her head.

With a sigh, she pushed off him and sat up. "I'm starving. Let's finish fixing this after dinner." She started to get to her feet, but, unwilling to let the moment pass, he sat up and wrapped his arms around her back. After a surprised second she slid her hands around his waist and caressed his back.

"Is it about this weekend?"

"This weekend?"

"You're worried about what we tell the gang?"

"Oh. Helping Jackson and Jordan move?"

"Yeah, I assumed you got asked, too."

She nodded. "So…what do you want to do?"

When he'd talked to Jackson the other night, he'd shaved every inch off the truth without actually lying to hide his affair with Alex. That way, if the whole thing went south, it wouldn't affect their friends. "Maybe we should keep…*us* a secret for now."

She tugged on her lower lip. "Sure. Just buddies. No problem." She met his gaze and smiled, but the smile misfired. Before he could stop her she lifted off him and started dressing.

What? Did she really want to announce to the world that they were lovers? Hadn't he just been thinking Hughes was the one person who came right out and said what was on her mind? With a sigh, he washed up and followed her into the kitchen.

Dinner was amazing. Tender roast. Buttery potatoes. Steamed vegetables and hot rolls. Mitch hadn't eaten a home-cooked meal like this in…he couldn't remember when. While they ate, they discussed football, their favorite college teams, the NFL teams, who was winning, who was losing, who they thought was going to the Super Bowl.

Feeling full and relaxed, Mitch leaned back, rubbing his stomach. "I didn't know you had this in your repertoire, Hughes."

"I told you that night in the officers' club." She leaned forward and propped her elbows on the table, one brow raised. "There's a lot about me you don't know."

He gave her a slow, seductive smile. "I'm enjoying what I've learned so far." He got up and stacked the dishes, then started rinsing and loading the dishwasher. The hairs on his neck rose as he felt Alex's eyes on him. He turned to find her staring at him.

"What?"

"I've never seen you wash dishes before."

He grinned. "I'm not a complete caveman." He reached for a dish. "When I was a kid, if I hadn't clea—" He froze.

"If you hadn't cleaned?" she prompted.

Mitch swallowed and made himself resume scrubbing a saucepan. "Let's just say my mom wasn't the best housekeeper." Hell, if that had been her only shortcoming, life might have been bearable. He felt Alex come up behind him and touch his back softly.

"Is that why your apartment and clothes are always spotless? Even your Jeep is immaculate."

He shrugged. "I guess."

She moved away, picking up a box of cereal he assumed had been left out from this morning. "And I'm such a slob." She rolled up the plastic bag inside and closed the lid before sticking it in the pantry.

"Hey." He stepped over and caught her around the waist, spinning her to face him. "Don't ever think you're anything close to being like my mom."

Her soft lips curved up in a smile and this time her eyes lit up, too. She cupped his cheek in her palm. "Thanks."

"I mean it, Alex. You're gorgeous, and intelligent, and...brave. Your courage has always amazed me."

Her brows rose. "I meant thanks for not deflecting and keeping it real about your mom."

"Oh." Why was that so important to her? She'd made a big deal of it at her painting party, too. Maybe he *could* talk to Alex about his past, up to a point. He trusted her more than anyone else he knew. And just now, instead of judging his mom, she'd seemed worried he would judge *her*.

Oh, well, he wasn't going to look a gift horse in the mouth. Returning her smile, he lowered his head and kissed her. "Maybe you should demonstrate your gratitude so I'll be encouraged to reveal more."

Her eyes widened. "Well, if I'd known that's all it took..." She cupped him over his zipper.

He lifted her to the counter. "Let me see that bra again."

Washing the dishes got put off and so did the bathroom pipe repair. They moved to the bedroom and

Mitch made sure Alex forgot everything except coming apart in his arms again and again.

Having taught her class last night and gotten up early to cook him dinner, she soon fell asleep on his shoulder as he lay there recovering from the huge orgasm that rocked him. Listening to her soft little snore, feelings came creeping over him, tender, mushy, urgent. He recognized it for what it was. Everything he'd thought he felt for Luanne. But deeper. Stronger. More real. More… terrifying.

13

ONCE AGAIN, SHE, Alexandria Annalise Hughes, had chickened out.

Last night she'd come so close to telling him that she loved him. She'd never thought of herself as a coward. And she knew eventually she'd have to get off the fence and, like her grandfather advised, go after that runaway calf. There was no way she would settle for half a relationship. But if she told Mitch she loved him, most likely his response would be that he loved having sex with her, and he really liked her a lot.

Besides the humiliation factor, there was the inevitable breakup. Once they split up, it wasn't that she would lose the man she loved. How could she lose something she'd never really had? No, the most painful thing would be losing her best friend. The one person who knew her, understood her and accepted her for who she was.

By eight the next morning she'd slipped out of

Mitch's arms, made coffee and driven to Jackson and Jordan's apartment.

Jordan put her to work wrapping items from the kitchen cabinets in newspaper and putting them in a box marked *Kitchen*. With Jordan in and out of the place supervising Jackson, who was disassembling the bed, Alex had too much time to think.

It hurt at first that Mitch wanted to keep their affair a secret. Was Mitch ashamed of their new relationship? Embarrassed to admit to his other buddies that they were sleeping together? But she could also see the wisdom of hiding their liaison. Fraternization between squadrons wasn't encouraged.

"Amazing how much stuff one accumulates after one gets married," Jordan said, wrapping a crystal compote. "We should've moved before the wedding."

"Jackson's family is nice, though," Alex responded. "Throwing you the shower and sending you guys on your honeymoon."

Jordan smiled, her eyes staring into the past. "They're wonderful. Growing up an only child, I always wanted siblings. And now I've instantly gained four of each. And his mom and dad, they're the best."

Alex thought about her folks and decided she'd try to get home for Thanksgiving. Considering she'd been trying to avoid spending time with her family most of her life, Jordan's situation made her realize how important her mom and dad, and even her brothers were to her. In their own way, they loved her. She knew that.

"Hey, babe, do you really want to keep this?" Jackson held up a faded Little Mermaid bedspread.

Jordan's cheeks pinkened. "That's my blankie. I really don't want to get rid of it." She turned to Alex. "My mom bought me the entire bed set for my fifth birthday. I realized years later she couldn't really afford it, but she'd worked a second job over Christmas to buy it."

"No worries, sweetheart. We'll save it for our kids, okay?" Jackson folded the spread and packed it in a box, all the while holding Jordan's gaze with that same look he'd given her at their wedding. That "You're the other half of my soul" look.

Alex got that same ache in her stomach. But she knew what it was now. An emptiness inside her, a longing for what Cole and Jordan had. They were talking about kids. A future. Together.

She remembered the night Jackson drove around looking for Jordan's mom after the woman—who had Alzheimer's—had run away. And ever since they'd been together, Jackson had been coming home from his night shift and caring for Jordan's mom during the day while Jordan worked, just to keep her mom out of a facility for as long as possible. Due to the advancing stages of the disease they'd recently been forced to move her mother to a long-term assisted living home. But they both visited every day.

That kind of devotion, that kind of commitment— Alex wanted that. She knew Mitch would do almost anything for her. But opening his heart up to love again? She swallowed a hard lump in her throat. That was the one thing he'd never do.

"Hey, sorry we're late." Lily walked into the tiny apartment, Grady right behind her. "I'm not moving very fast in the mornings lately." She rubbed her stomach.

Grady slipped an arm around her shoulders. "I don't know how women go through all this."

Lily glanced up at him with that expectant glow. "Just six more months, honey. Then we'll have a beautiful baby to show for it."

Alex spun on her heels and reached blindly into a cabinet for something to pack. The love in this apartment was suffocating.

"Okay, I'm here. Put me to work." At the sound of Mitch's voice Alex jerked and almost dropped the Viva Las Vegas vase she'd grabbed from the cabinet.

Apparently everyone else was just as shocked as she was. A stunned moment of silence permeated the room as Alex turned to take in her lover.

"What?" Mitch held a tray full of Styrofoam cups of expensive coffee in one hand and a box from a doughnut shop in the other. He hadn't shaved, and he was wearing the same shorts and shirt he'd left at her house. Only Mitchell McCabe could manage to make scruffy look sexy.

"Kind of early for you, McCabe," Jackson said as

he stood, took the box of doughnuts and shook Mitch's right hand.

Mitch's gaze slid to Alex and she quickly resumed wrapping the vase and packing it in a box.

"I owe a forfeit, I pay it in full," Mitch said. "I brought coffee." He lifted the tray with a smile.

"Oh, dear." Lily clamped a hand over her mouth and went running down the hall.

Grady winced. "Coffee's one of the smells that sends her hurling." He strode after her.

Poor Mitch. His smile faded as he lowered the tray of drinks. "Sorry about that."

"No, no." Jordan grabbed the tray. "Smells heavenly to me." She took a cup and sipped some coffee. "We rented a trailer, but we had to park it at the end of the lot. How about you guys start loading furniture while us gals finish packing?"

"Sounds good," Jackson agreed. "McCabe, you want to grab the other end of the sofa?"

"Sure." Mitch darted another glance at Alex before bending to lift the sofa and followed Jackson out.

"What was that all about?" Jordan asked as soon as the guys were out the door.

"What?" Alex kept her attention on packing.

"Are you and Mitch quarrelling?"

Alex assumed her most innocent expression. "McCabe and me? No."

"Then what was with all the furtive glances and the silence? You didn't give him a hard time about being out all night with some new bimbo now that his thirty days is up? Or make some snarky wisecrack about him making Lily puke?"

Alex scoffed. "My world doesn't revolve around Mi—McCabe. I have a life." Crap, that came out too defensive.

After Jordan didn't respond, Alex finally looked up.

Jordan was staring at her, scrutinizing, calculating.

Feeling her face heating, Alex spun to grab something else out of a cabinet.

"Oh. My. God," Jordan gasped.

Alex gritted her teeth and turned back around.

"You're sleeping with him!" Jordan looked horrified.

"You say that like I was sleeping with a terrorist or something."

Just then Grady and Lily returned from the bathroom. Grady was shaking his head. Obviously, they'd overheard. "Damn it, Hughes."

Lily shrugged one shoulder. "I told you. Their auras were both so red." At least she was smiling. "And I, for one, am happy for you, Alex."

"Oh, Alex." Jordan shook her head, sympathy in her eyes.

"What?" Alex challenged. "What's the big deal?"

"What goes next, hon?" Jackson appeared in the doorway, Mitch behind him.

Everyone jumped and looked guilty at Jackson's question. Good grief. What was this? *As the Air Combat Instructor's World Turns?*

"Well, Jackson." Alex stomped past Jordan to stand nose to nose with her old friend. "You might as well know the whole sordid truth. McCabe and I are shagging each other's brains out. We're doing the dirty. Burying the bone. Glazing the doughnut. Dipping the corn dog in the batter. We can't keep our hands off each other!"

Poor Jackson just raised his brows and propped his fists on his hips. "Con...gratulations?"

Mitch pushed past Jackson, put his arm around Alex's shoulders. "Don't worry, my fragile flower, I'll protect you from these Puritans." Then he spoke low into her ear. "What finally broke you, soldier? Was it the newlywed couples' love-fest? Or were you subjected to twenty-four hours of Yanni?"

She elbowed him in the gut and folded her arms across her chest.

"Oomph!" Mitch grabbed his stomach. "Come on, Hughes, I'm still sore there."

A high giggle came from Lily and Alex glanced over at her. She was covering her mouth, laughing, and Alex spluttered into laughter, too. Jordan broke next, and soon they were all chuckling.

Mitch put both arms around Alex and took possession of her mouth in a deep, long kiss. She threw her arms around his neck and kissed him back, matching him tongue for tongue, moan for moan.

When he slowly released her, he whispered, "Are they all watching?"

She glanced around and then nodded.

"Good." He grinned and looked around the room. "Any questions?"

"Um…you want to help Cole take out the TV?" Jordan answered.

With the tension broken, everything went back to normal. Alex was still embarrassed thinking about her outburst. But thankfully Mitch's sense of humor had dispelled the charged silence.

By the time the sun was setting the apartment was empty and the last run had been made to Jackson and Jordan's new house. It was a mansion compared to Alex's cozy two-bedroom, but then, they planned on having lots of kids. Alex got a little knot in her stomach thinking about that. She'd changed so much from that militant eighteen-year-old at the academy.

Now that her career was for the most part established, and the man she loved wanted kids so badly—at least, he used to—she wouldn't mind considering having a family. But after all these years of watching Mitch nurse the pain of Luanne's betrayal, Alex would have to be a bubble-headed Pollyanna to believe he could truly love her, much less want to be in a committed relationship. So she shoved the idea way down deep, like she did everything lately.

Jackson declared tomorrow a day of rest, except coming over for barbecued ribs. Jordan hugged everyone and thanked them, and soon Mitch was following Alex back to her house.

As soon as his Jeep came to a stop behind her Mustang, he jumped out and swung her up into his arms. "I don't know what made you decide to tell everyone, but I'm kind of glad to have it out in the open."

"I didn't *decide* to tell them— You are?" Alex wanted to pinch herself.

He set her down and took the keys from her hand. "Yep. I can't stand lying."

"Me, either."

Unlocking the door, he took her hand and pulled her inside. "I know. And I love that you hate lying, and I love that I know that about you." Who was this man and what had he done with Mitch?

"Really? Alex entered her house feeling as if she were in an alternate universe.

"Really." He pulled his T-shirt off, toed out of his shoes and headed for the bathroom. "And since our secret's out—" he turned and walked backward while he talked "—I think we should make plans to go out somewhere fun with our married friends next weekend after our promotion ceremony."

"You *do?*" Alex's eyes couldn't get any wider. But a seed of cautious optimism took root inside her.

"I do." He raised his brows and dropped his shorts. "Coming to shower?" He flashed those adorable dimples, turned and disappeared into the bathroom.

In a daze, Alex followed slowly. Could they be a real couple? Have a real relationship? She shed her clothes, stepped into the shower and wound her arms around his waist. "When you say 'somewhere fun,' that doesn't mean dragsters and dollar beers, does it?"

SITUATION REPORT: HEADED for Uncharted Territory.

Shirt by shirt, razor to toothbrush to cologne, over the next few days, Mitch began leaving his things at Alex's. Since she was still on night maneuvers, the only way to maximize his time with her was to go ahead and spend the night there during the week, too.

The change seemed barely discernible. Alex made room for his stuff on the bathroom counter, in her closet and drawers, and they even talked about bringing his big-screen TV over for watching games on the weekends.

So, it seemed without either of them discussing it, he'd—for all intents and purposes—moved in with Alex. If anyone had told him a month ago he'd be moving in with a woman, he'd have laughed and denied it with every fiber of his being. He might have even made another stupid bet like he had when Jackson had talked about marrying Jordan. That's how sure he'd been then.

Now, uncertainty seemed to have moved into his psyche and made itself right at home alongside the bit of terror that still remained. All he knew was that, despite the fear, he was happy, and that a part of him he thought had died, the part that believed in love, that needed love, wasn't dead.

It was on life support and needed a lot of intensive care.

But for the first time in more than seven long years, his heart was cautiously, one wonderful day at a time, coming back to life. And it felt good.

He decided to come clean with Commander Westland, but he had to let Hughes know his plans first. It wouldn't prevent him or her from receiving a promotion, but it might mean reassignment for one or both of them.

Following the advice of his administrative assistant, he had a friend of his get front-row tickets for the whole gang to one of the Cirque du Soleil shows on the strip for Saturday night. The plan was to surprise everyone with the tickets after the ceremony on base Saturday.

By lunchtime Friday he was too excited to wait to tell Alex about the show. He decided to take off early, buy himself a new shirt, and then surprise Alex at home with the tickets.

He didn't know which one he was more excited about: he and Alex getting promoted to the rank of major, or he and Alex making it official that they were a couple.

Somehow the two seemed connected in his mind. Maybe because whenever something good had happened in his life, Alex was always a part of it.

14

ALEX JERKED AWAKE as her cell phone played "Anchors Aweigh." She grabbed the phone off her bedside table. "Hughes."

"Alexandria, hey. It's Neil."

Alex swiped the hair out of her mouth and blinked the sleep from her eyes. Neil. She hadn't heard his deep voice in over a year. A vivid memory assaulted her of Neil's delighted expression when he realized she'd used the Navy's theme song as his ringtone on her cell.

She cleared her throat. "Yeah, hey, hi, Neil. How're you doing?" She rolled over and sat up, checking her alarm clock. Noon? She'd had three hours of sleep. But that wasn't Neil's fault. He didn't know she was on night maneuvers.

"—you out to lunch?"

"Wait, what?"

"I'm sorry. You sound like you're not feeling well. Is this a bad time?"

"I was asleep. I'm on night duty this rotation."

"Oh, no, I woke you up? I'm so sorry."

"No problem. What were you saying?"

"I'm in town and thought I'd take you out to lunch, but it sounds like that's not going to work for you."

"Oh, yeah, I'm not really fit for public consumption right now." She gave a short laugh that died in the silence.

"Well, listen, I'm on leave and I flew in to Vegas because I wanted to see you. Maybe I could come over there later this afternoon? After you get a few hours' more sleep."

"Uh…" He flew in just to see her? Hadn't she made it clear before she left Langley that they were done as a couple?

"I know it's rude to invite myself over, but I'm shipping out next week and I thought I'd see how you're doing before I go."

"No, no problem. Come on by. I just bought a house." She rattled off the address.

"If you're sure?"

"Yeah, it'd be nice to catch up." That's all this was. Two friends catching up after a year.

"Great. Be there in about an hour."

After Alex clicked off, she jumped in the shower, blew her hair dry and tried to apply a little makeup, but her hand shook. Why was she so nervous? She cared about Neil, but she certainly didn't love him.

She dashed into the living room, madly snatching

up clothes, trash and takeout boxes. She'd be so embarrassed to let Neil see the way she lived. Heading to the kitchen, she stopped in her tracks. Why did it matter if Neil saw the way she lived, but not Mitch? *Think about that later, Hughes.*

The kitchen was a mess. She stuffed things anywhere they'd fit, cabinets, pantry, the fridge, and then cleaned all the surfaces with bacteria-killing disposable wipes.

As she cleaned, it occurred to her, it'd been over a year since she'd felt compelled to try to impress someone, to be on her best behavior. To be someone she wasn't.

And she didn't miss feeling that way.

She'd once met his father, stumbled over her words and ended up using profanity. Neil had said he thought it was cute, but cute only went so far before it became annoying to someone with his kind of background. She could just hear the senator talking to his colleagues. *Yes, my son's in the navy, but his date's the one who swears like a sailor.*

She cringed at the memory.

Neil didn't know she was a world-title-holder slob. Or that she snored like a chainsaw grinding through redwood.

The doorbell rang and she jumped, her heart racing. Taking a deep breath, she smoothed her hands down her jeans and went to get the door.

As soon as she swung it open, his classy cologne hit her senses. But as expensive as she knew it was, it didn't do a thing for her. "Hey." She smiled and offered her cheek as he bent down to hug her and kissed the corner of her mouth.

"Hi." He wore his service dress uniform, shiny shoes, and ribbons covering his suit coat pocket. "Housewarming gift." Bowing slightly from the waist, he presented her with an expensive bottle of wine, mimicking a maître d' at an expensive restaurant.

"Oh, you didn't have to do that." She took the wine and stepped back, gesturing him inside. "I thought I'd make tuna salad. You want a sandwich?"

"Whatever you make is great." He followed her into the kitchen and stood at the counter while she pulled out a can of tuna.

He was taller than Mitch, broader. At five feet three inches, she felt like a dwarf next to him. He made her nervous just standing there watching her. Did he notice the awkwardness between them like she did?

"Your house is nice," he finally said.

"Thanks. It's just an old fixer-upper, but I like the classic fifties details, like the built-in shelf in the hallway for the phone."

"Oh?"

"Yeah, and the original wood trim along the front gable? They don't make 'em like that anymore." Oh, God, she was rambling. She glanced over at him and smiled.

He returned it. "Hey, can I help with anything?"

"Oh, nah. Not much to do." She pulled mayo from the

fridge. "You like celery or pickles in your tuna salad?" She wouldn't have had to ask Mitch that. She knew already. To be fair, she'd known him longer. But she'd dated Neil almost two years. She'd slept with the man, for crying out loud. She should know how he liked his tuna.

"Either is fine." He just stood there and watched her.

"Have a seat and tell me how the hell— How are you? You're shipping out, huh?" She knew not to ask him where. He probably couldn't say.

As she chopped an onion, boiled a couple of eggs and mixed everything in a bowl, he sat, crossed his legs in that upper-class elegant way of his and talked.

He kept the conversation light, filling her in on all of their mutual friends in D.C. He talked of his father and mother, and their busy lives, and told her of a lady, a young lobbyist, he'd been dating a few months.

Alex made the sandwiches, set his on a plate before him with some sliced apples and pulled out a bag of potato chips.

"This looks wonderful." He smiled down at the food and then back up at her. "I think that's what I've always liked about you. You're so down-to-earth." He picked up the sandwich and took a man-size bite.

She blinked. Down-to-earth? Was that code for unsophisticated? Uncouth? "Gee, you really know how to flatter a girl, Neil."

His eyes widened and he stopped chewing. Swallowing quickly, he shook his head. "No, I— That came out wrong. I meant it as a compliment. Truly."

Feeling bad for the poor guy, she smiled. "I know. Don't worry about it."

He cleared his throat, scooted back in the chair, and stood. "Restroom?"

"Uh…" She scrambled up from her seat and motioned him out of the kitchen and to the right. Oh, crud, had she straightened up the bathroom? "The door on the right."

She busied herself searching the pantry for anything she could offer for dessert besides a half-eaten bag of Oreos. As she heard the water running, she poured them both a glass of iced tea and then paced the kitchen. Why was he really here? Maybe he was marrying that lobbyist and wanted to let Alex know personally. But she'd made it clear when she left D.C. that she was breaking up with him. Maybe—

She spun on her heel as he appeared in the kitchen. "Want some tea?" She held out the glass to him.

"No, thanks." He shoved his hands in his slacks pockets and gazed out the window above her sink to the backyard. "Is that a pool?"

"Yes!" She seized on the topic for conversation. "It's small but it comes in handy in this desert heat."

He was still gazing out the window. "It's nice out today. Not too hot, not too cold."

No way he came here just to talk about the weather. "Would you like to sit outside?"

"Yes." His smile looked relieved as he swung his gaze back to her.

She stepped around the table, opened the back door and led him out to the patio.

"It's beautiful out here," Neil said from behind her. "You've done a great job on the landscaping."

"Well, I had help." Sipping her tea, she surveyed the flowerbeds and remembered the day Mitch had helped her plant them all. What a great time they'd had that day.

"Alexandria." He caught her gaze. "I didn't come here just to catch up on old times."

Oh, no. She wanted to run back in the house, but she made herself stay put. "You didn't?"

He shook his head. "No."

She opened her mouth, but he stopped her. "Look. I haven't been able to stop thinking about you. The truth is, I still have feelings for you, and I came here to see if there was any way, before I shipped out, that you'd want to give us another try."

As much as she should've seen this coming, she was still stunned into silence. To camouflage her surprise, she turned and set her tea down on the table, then forced herself to face him. "Did you know I snore so loud it rivals an F-16 buzzing the house?"

Neil frowned. "You never snored when we were together."

"That's because I never let myself fall asleep after..." She waved a hand. "You know."

"You didn't?"

"No, and I never let you see my apartment unless I'd cleaned it first. I'm a horrible slob."

He shrugged. "Well, nobody's perfect."

"And did you know I've assaulted two fellow officers in the past month? I have a wicked temper. When I get really mad, I don't care about the consequences."

Neil frowned. "You're deliberately trying to scare me off. Why?"

"Not scare you off. Just show you the real me. I made the mistake of not doing that with you, Neil. You're such a great guy. And I wanted things to work out between us so badly. I...needed to be in a normal relationship." She stuck her hands in her back pockets and studied her unpainted toenails. "I thought I was being honest with you when we met. Telling you I'd requested the transfer to get away from a guy who didn't return my love. I thought with sheer will I could make myself love someone else and be happy."

Looking back up, she stared into his serious, dark brown eyes. "I didn't realize I was only fooling myself. You've heard the saying, 'The heart wants what the heart wants'?" She gave a one-shouldered shrug.

"So." He stepped close, brought his hand up and ran a thumb over her cheek. "Did things work out with this guy? Are you happy now?"

She made herself smile and covered his hand with hers. "After everything I told you, you're worried about me?"

He returned her smile. "I love you, Alexandria. I want you to be happy."

"Oh, Neil." She slid her arms around his waist and hugged him, her cheek flattened against his chest. "Why couldn't I have loved you?" she mumbled to herself.

Neil squeezed her to him a moment then pulled away and held her shoulders. "So, the idiot came to his senses?"

She couldn't meet his gaze. "I don't know."

He crooked a finger under her chin and lifted her face to him. "If he doesn't, and you change your mind…" He slowly bent down and touched his lips to hers. His kiss was achingly sweet, and then he raised his head. "Contact me through my dad. Okay?"

She nodded. He was such a nice g—

The front door slammed shut and she jerked her gaze to the back door. Neil hadn't closed it behind him. Anyone standing in the shadow of the kitchen would've seen Neil kiss her.

She heard the familiar roar of Mitch's Jeep's engine firing up and cursed long and loudly. As tires screeched in her driveway, she ran for the front door and out into the front yard just in time to see Mitch's Jeep careen around the corner in a spray of gravel.

Suddenly, she remembered Lily's warning about sea animals. A seal was a sea animal.

If the whole thing weren't so disastrous, she'd have chuckled.

15

SITUATION REPORT: ON the way to getting totally shit-faced.

Mitch snagged a barstool in the seediest dive he could find in Vegas. The floor was sticky with who knew what. The air held the vague odor of urine and vomit. No chance of anyone he knew locating him here. He'd turned his cell off after ignoring the third call from Alex.

Alex! He kept picturing her in that navy man's arms, kissing him…

Goddammit! The one person he'd always believed he could trust. Who'd never lie to him or go behind his back.

Country music blared from a battered jukebox, and an old Haggard song was playing, something about turning off the memories.

If only he could.

But that's what he'd come here for.

A hulking man behind the bar looked at him questioningly.

"A bottle of Jim Beam."

Without batting an eye the bartender grabbed a bottle and a shot glass, opened the bottle, and set it on the bar in front of Mitch.

Mitch laid a fifty on the bar. "I'm going to need a bigger glass." In his uniform, and wearing his Tag Heuer watch and diamond tiepin, he might not look like he fit in here. But this was exactly the kind of place he belonged. Only the truly down-and-out patronized this seedy joint. The ones who'd given up on life a long time ago and were just waiting to die. People like his mother.

Once the barkeep handed him a large tumbler, Mitch filled it and raised the glass in a silent toast to dear old mom. *To Angi McCabe. Whoever you're spreading your legs for tonight, I hope he pays you enough to score your next hit.* Knocking back the bourbon in one gulp, he slammed the glass on the counter and poured himself another.

His mom. Last time he'd seen her, he'd just been promoted to First Lieutenant, and he'd been saving his money for a while. He used his leave before shipping out to Iraq to fly to Memphis, making sure to wear his service dress uniform with his ribbons.

He took her out to dinner and offered to pay for a rehab facility close to where he'd be stationed when he got back. She'd seemed so happy to see him. So eager to get clean and sober.

He'd told her he'd bought her a ticket to Vegas, and gave her some money for food—she looked so thin. She'd promised to go. He'd made plans to pick her up at her trailer the next morning.

But when he got there, the first thing he saw was a brand-new case of whiskey on the floor under the table. His blood ran cold and he called for his ma, but she didn't answer. So, he stumbled back to the bedroom and she was lying there, stinking drunk with some low-life passed out beside her.

Disgusted, Mitch strode back to the table, grabbed up the case of whiskey and tried to take it outside. But the man must have been more awake than he looked. He'd caught up to Mitch at the door and hit him across the back with a two-by-four.

His mom was screaming, not telling the old guy to stop hitting Mitch, no. She was screaming at Mitch, begging him to leave them alone.

He hadn't let himself think about his mom in a long time. But tonight he couldn't seem to stop the memories.

The bourbon roiled in his gut.

That's what he needed. A woman. He looked around the bar. The only female in here was on her knees under the back booth earning her booze in a time-honored tradition. Okay, he hadn't sunk that low. He'd never paid for it. And he never ever would.

Refilling the tumbler, he went to work draining the bottle of Jim Beam. He eyed the bartender, wondering if he should trust him with his keys to the Jeep and to call him a cab. He couldn't guarantee he'd be this sensible later. The drunker he got, the cockier he might get about being able to drive.

Mitch pulled his wallet out and slid a fifty and his keys over to the burly, bald dude serving drinks. "Can I trust you to keep these locked up and call me a cab when closing time comes?"

The bartender's gaze darted from the money and keys up to Mitch. He could've sworn he saw a spark of respect in the guy's eyes before he nodded and snatched them off the bar.

Hey, say anything you want about Mitch McCabe. He may be a drunk and a whore's son, but he wasn't no drunk driver.

He poured himself more bourbon and drank it down until the bottle was empty and he had to ask for a new one. But his lips wouldn't form the words. His vision got blurry and the room started swaying, so he laid his head down on the bar for a few minutes. When he lifted his head he knew he had to be totally plastered because he was having a hallucination.

He saw Alex come in the door and scan the place until her gaze landed on him. Then she headed straight for him.

Uh-oh. She looked mad. He laughed. Wouldn't it piss her off if he said she looked beautiful when she was mad? Wait. Had he already said that to her one time? He couldn't remember. Didn't matter. Even with her hair looking like she'd run her hands through it a hundred times, this hallucination Alex was gorgeous.

As she came up alongside him and leaned on the bar, her expression changed from mad to sad. Good. He was the one who should be mad. He'd tell her, too. Except he couldn't remember what he was mad about.

"Oh, Mitch." She cupped his face in her hands and searched his eyes.

"Hello, Alexandria. I'm very mad at you."

"I know, but you didn't see what you thought you saw."

"I didn't?" Thinking about that sentence made his head hurt. He squeezed his eyes shut. What did he not see? He was so confused.

"No, you idiot." Her hands slid down to his shoulders. "Neil only came to—"

"That was it!" He tried to snap his fingers but they wouldn't snap. "I was mad at Alex for kissing Neil-the-SEAL."

"It's not what you think. He's shipping out next week."

"Off to earn another medal, I bet. No wonder Alex kissed him. She deserves a guy like that." He looked up at the hallucination.

"I don't want him. I want you, Mitch."

Of course his hallucination would say that. But the real Alex would choose Neil-the-SEAL. Seeing the guy in person only brought home how perfect he was. Tall, dark and handsome. And Alex had her arms wrapped around him, looking at him like he'd just brought about world peace and ended world hunger all at once.

"Nah. She doesn't want me. Why should she? My mother's a whore and so am I." He glanced at Hallucination Alex. "I know that's what she really thinks. She doesn't like me anymore, that's why she went away to D.C. in the first place. She used to think I was a great guy." He stared down into his drink. "But not anymore. I'm just a good lay."

He wiped a hand over his mouth. "I bet Mr. Perfect Neil-the-SEAL sent her cards and flowers all the time. And he'd never go three days without calling her."

"Oh, Mitch." Her hands came back up to his face and she leaned in to give him a soft kiss.

"I like it when you kiss me, Alex." He smiled. Then he frowned. "The real Alex is kissing Neil-the-SEAL."

"I am not."

He closed his eyes and placed his forehead against hers. "Want something to drink?"

"Mitch, I want you to come home with me now, okay?"

He shook his head but that made the room really start spinning. "Not driving. Calling a cab."

"Well, that's good, but I can drive you. Come on." She took his arm and it felt so real.

He laughed again. "Silly girl. Hallucinations can't drive."

"Mitch, I'm not a hallucination. I'm really here. But you can't stay here like this. How do think you're going to get to the ceremony tomorrow if you're passed-out drunk?"

"Ceremony?" A vague recollection of something special going on tomorrow tickled his brain. "What ceremony? I'm not getting married, am I? No way! I'll never get married again. Luanne cheated. Alex cheated." He looked at hallucination Alex. "Why'd you cheat on me, Alex?" He curled his hands into fists and stuck his fists on the counter. "I wanted to kill that SOB. Kissing *my* girl. She was mine."

"Mitch, get your ass up." She lifted his arm around her shoulders and hauled him off the stool. "We're leaving."

He stood. Maybe he could hallucinate one more night with Alex.

"That's it. Can you walk?"

Of course he could walk. Whoa, good thing she was holding on to him. She was strong, holding him up with her shoulder tucked under his arm.

Hey, when did it get dark out? Had he been here that long? What was it he was supposed to do tomorrow?

"There we go." He felt himself sliding down into a bucket seat. "Now let's get your seat belt on." Alex's voice sounded so nice. But she was mad at him, wasn't she? No. Wait. *He* was mad at *her*. And he'd tell her so as soon as the entire world stopped spinning.

As she got in and drove the car out of the parking lot, he leaned his head back against the headrest and closed his eyes.

When he woke up the car had stopped and Hallucination Alex helped him get out of the car and walk to her door. Wait. He didn't want to be here. "No." He stopped. "Doan wanna be here." He yanked his arm from her grasp and turned back toward the car.

"Wait. Mitch. Where are you going?" She caught his arm and tugged him back. Damn, she was strong. "Come on. Come to bed with me."

How could he resist her? He thought he nodded, but he wasn't sure if maybe that was just the ground moving. "Okay."

Somehow he made it back to her bedroom and fell on the bed. But the room kept spinning. Then she was tugging on him, pulling off his shoes and socks and pants. Tugging his arms out of his coat and loosening his tie, and unbuttoning his shirt. Her hands caressed his chest and it felt so good. He grinned.

"Mmm, baby, come here." He reached for her and yanked her down on top of him. Yeah, he liked sleeping with her in his arms. He remembered that. He remembered this feeling. The feeling of rightness.

He was forgetting something, but he'd think about that later. Right now, he'd snuggle with Alex...

ALEX LAY AWAKE a long time holding Mitch. She couldn't believe she'd found him. Well, the cops had found him for her.

She must have driven around every hotel casino parking garage on the strip looking for his Jeep. She'd finally called Jackson and asked him to ask his friends on the force to be on the lookout for the Jeep.

The last time she'd seen Mitch this drunk was the night he'd come to her after he caught Luanne cheating on him. He'd only been married six months. He'd been so devastated, so hurt. But he'd called her, Alex. Needing her to listen, to comfort, and to assure him he would survive the pain.

She'd seen the softer side of Mitch that night. And she'd fallen even more in love with him.

But this time he hadn't had her to come to. He'd had to go to a place like that.

Mitch rolled to his back and gasped in pain. He grabbed his head, then spotted her and groaned. "So you were real."

Alex rose up onto an elbow. "You want some coffee? Or are you going to be sick?"

He sat up slowly and swung his legs off the bed. "Going home."

"Mitch, we need to talk."

"No, we don't." He stood, gingerly walked to the chest of drawers and opened the drawer she'd given him for his clothes.

"You're not in any condition to drive. And even if you were, your Jeep is still at that bar."

He stopped in the middle of pulling up some jeans. "Then I'll call a cab."

"Mitch, Neil was—"

"You really don't want to say his name to me right

now," he snarled as he zipped his jeans. He glanced back at her. "You know what my problem is? I gotta quit coming home early." He let out a humorless laugh. "Or maybe it's thinking I even have a home."

"Mitch, I was only telling him that I couldn't be with him."

"Yeah." He yanked a T-shirt over his head. "I could tell from that kiss."

"That was a 'Goodbye, have a nice life' kiss."

"You know what?" He swiveled to face her. "Why should I care? We were just fuck-buddies, right?"

A sharp pain stabbed her as if a saber had just pierced her chest. If he'd meant to hurt her, he'd succeeded splendidly.

She bit down hard on the inside of her cheek. "I *love* you, you moron."

"Yeah, well, baby, I don't *do* love." He slid his sneakers on. "Love is for suckers. I told you that."

She scrambled off the bed and blocked his way out of the bedroom. "I don't believe you."

"I tried the white picket fence, and the two-point-five-kids route. I was all in. Thought I'd live happily ever after. And what did it get me? A cheating wife and court-ordered spousal support for a year. That's what love gets you, Hughes." He was bitter, sneering.

No matter how many times she'd imagined Mitch saying exactly that when she told him she loved him, it still felt like a physical blow to the chest. She'd known this would be the result. His thinking she was a cheater like Luanne only accelerated the inevitable outcome. She'd lost her best friend. The one person she counted on to make her feel better when life got hard.

Now who would she turn to?

"Goodbye, Hughes." He grabbed his cell phone off the bedside table, stepped around her and called a cab.

Eyes stinging, Alex raced out to the backyard, around the pool to the far edge of her property and sank down against the fence. She couldn't be in that house while Mitch gathered all his things and left in a cab. She pulled her knees up, lowered her head, but her eyes remained dry. She refused to cry over Mitch.

In a few hours she'd have to attend a ceremony in her formal dress uniform, step forward and receive her promotion to major next to the man who used to be her best buddy but now hated her. No way she'd get back to sleep. But she was pretty sure the stuff she'd bought during her makeover included some sort of eye cream. At least she wouldn't have to stand in front of everyone with puffy red eyes.

And that mundane kind of thinking and performing those kinds of everyday tasks was the only thing that got her through the next twelve hours.

16

SITUATION REPORT: PROMOTED today.

This should be the happiest day of his life. His career was all he had. All he'd ever had. If he wasn't a U.S. Air Force officer, he was nothing.

So why did Mitch feel like nothing anyway?

As he looked out over the small gathering, it seemed everyone's families surrounded them. Wives, husbands, kids. Even Hughes's mother and father had flown up to surprise her. She'd started freakin' crying when she saw them out in the audience. He'd never seen Hughes cry. And he'd never seen her look more beautiful.

He had no one here.

Sure, Jackson had shown up. But he was here just as much for Alex. And Grady had to be here. He was Alex's commander.

The ceremony was hard to get through. At 1350 the thirty-some-odd guests were asked to be seated. At 1400 Lieutenant Colonel Grady approached the podium.

"Good afternoon. Thank you for joining us today as we recognize two of our own, Captain Alexandria Hughes and Captain Mitchell McCabe, on the occasion of their promotion to major.

"Captain McCabe and Captain Hughes are two of the finest officers of any squadron I've had the privilege to serve with. They approach both combat and instructing with the highest level of integrity and honor. Their commitment and dedication is truly inspiring.

"And now, to officiate today's ceremony, ladies and gentlemen, Commander Westland."

Colonel Westland entered the room and stopped in front of the row of flags. He made a brief speech about his pride in his elite team of air-combat instructors. Mitch quit listening. It felt like Westland was talking about someone else. Someone Mitch didn't even know.

Grady called attention to orders. "The president of the United States, acting upon the recommendation of the secretary of the air force, has placed special trust and confidence in the patriotism, integrity and abilities of Captains Hughes and McCabe."

"In view of these special qualities, Captains Hughes and McCabe are promoted to the grade of Major, United States Air Force, by order of the secretary of the Air Force."

Colonel Westland stepped forward and pinned on their new ranks and then stepped to their side for photographs while the audience applauded. Then Westland asked him and Hughes to raise their right hands and administered the oath of office.

After he and Hughes uttered, "So help me God," Westland declared the ceremony concluded and invited everyone to stay for the reception following in the officers' club.

Mitch should've been over-the-moon thrilled. He should've been grinning and shaking his friends' hands. Having them clap him on the back.

He should've been hugging Alex. Kissing her. They should've been celebrating together.

Instead, she'd turned away from him and walked out to greet her parents and Jackson and Jordan. Hugging them all. What the…? Neil-the-SEAL approached Hughes and her parents. Hugged her. Shook her dad's hand.

She should've been introducing *him* to them. Not the SEAL.

But after last night? It was over.

When he saw Jackson and Grady heading toward him, he knew he had to get out of here. He didn't want to deal with them right now.

He ducked out a side door and headed down a hallway. His walk turned into a jog as he raced down a corridor and found a door leading out.

On the way there this afternoon, he'd had to take a cab to the bar where he'd left his Jeep last night. They'd just barely opened when he got there. The same bartender was there and handed him his keys from the safe in the back.

Glad to have his own transportation, he strode around the corner outside the building, found his Jeep and jumped in. Keys in hand, he started the engine and tore out of the parking lot and off base.

What he needed right now was anonymity. And he wouldn't get that in his uniform. At his apartment, he changed into jeans and a dress shirt. As he hung his uniform jacket in the closet, he studied the new ribbon on the pocket.

He was Major Mitch McCabe now. A corner of his mouth turned up at the alliteration. Today, he'd achieved a goal he'd had since joining the air force. He ran his fingers over the ribbon, searching for the joy, the pride, the sense of triumph. But he felt none of those things. The damn promotion didn't mean a thing to him without... He swallowed, hung the jacket up, and got out of his apartment.

Sitting on a stool at his favorite bar at the MGM Grand Hotel, the Centrifuge, he ordered a beer on tap and turned to scan the hotel's patrons. The bar was mostly empty at three in the afternoon, but the casino itself was busy as always. He spotted a couple of prospects for companionship and observed them for a while, deciding on his next move.

This was what Casanova McCabe did. What he was good at. He'd been happy before. Nobody messing with his psyche, making him think he needed them to be happy. He had to get his mojo back. Had to be that guy again.

And he would. As soon as he made sure the two women were alone. Casanova McCabe didn't poach. And he might as well finish this beer before he approached them. Besides, there was a game on the television above the bar.

He nursed the beer, kept his eye on the women and watched the game. After his second beer, he realized he'd lost sight of the women. No big deal. Plenty of fish where they came from.

He swung around on his stool and scouted the area, searching for a voluptuous blonde.

"Target sighted?" Jackson said, coming up next to him.

Mitch jumped and swiveled toward his friend. Grady stood behind Jackson, who was still in his suit and tie. Grady was still in his uniform. "What are you guys doing here?"

Jackson grinned and clapped him on the shoulder. "You didn't give us a chance to congratulate you."

Grady nodded his way. "Major McCabe."

"What are *you* doing here, McCabe?" Jackson took the stool next to him, made eye contact with the bartender and ordered a beer. Grady ordered water. "Looking for a female to help you celebrate?"

Mitch narrowed his eyes. "Abso-freakin'-lutely."

"So?" Jackson nudged him. "*Do* you have a target sighted?"

Mitch shrugged. "Maybe." Damn. His chest tightened, ready to explode. This was where it had all started. With Jackson seeing Jordan across the casino and deciding he was going to get her into his bed. If only they'd gone to the Bellagio that night. "I wish I'd never made that ridiculous bet with you, Jackson."

"Hey, that turned out to be the best thing I ever did."

"Best thing for me, too, Major," Grady broke in. "If I hadn't lost and you hadn't suggested I get that massage, my life would be empty right now."

Mitch grunted. "You're both still in the honeymoon stage."

Jackson glanced at Grady, and a look passed between them. Great. Here came the lecture about love being painful, but worth it. Well, they could take their lecture and—"

"I thought you handled losing the bet pretty well, other than Hughes's prank." Jackson nudged Grady and winked. "Remember those women showing up on base? Hughes got you good arranging for all your exes to visit you."

"Maybe I handled it too well," Mitch mumbled, and then grimaced. Why had he said that?

Jackson frowned, scrutinizing him like he was a perp in an interrogation room. "What does that mean?"

"Nothing." Mitch took a sip of his beer.

Grady and Jackson exchanged another look between them, which was getting irritating.

Then Jackson grimaced and folded his arms across

his chest. "I can't believe I'm about to say this, except that I've found it to be true with my wife, but you might feel better if you talk about it."

Mitch raised his brows. He couldn't believe his friend the cop had said that, either. But what did it matter?

"It means I wasn't that miserable that first time. Things had become…routine. I tried getting back to normal when my thirty days were up, but it just wasn't the same. I didn't enjoy it anymore."

"And this last time?" Jackson prompted.

Mitch remembered that first night after Jackson's wedding. His smug confidence that this time it would be even easier. Then he'd seen Alex in that red dress and his world had shifted. Nothing was the same after that. Unwilling to discuss Alex and that entire situation, he just shrugged.

"It was Hughes, wasn't it?" Grady asked.

Mitch studied the foam in his beer. "I liked her better when she wasn't a woman."

Jackson frowned. "Wasn't a woman?"

"You know, before she changed. When she was one of us."

Grady sputtered, "McCabe. She's always been female."

"Well, ever since she started acting like one, she's been messing with my head."

Jackson nodded. "A woman will do that to you."

Grady leaned his elbows on the bar. "Isn't that the truth."

All three nodded, taking sips of their drinks, turning their attention to the game until the next commercial.

Mitch turned to face his buddies. "So you guys know what I'm talking about. One minute she acts like she wants to crawl into my shorts, and the next she's punching me in the gut."

Jackson nodded again. "Logic isn't their strong suit."

"Logic?" Grady retorted. "Lily wouldn't know logical if it bit her very fine ass."

Jackson grinned. "Jordan thinks me being logical is a bad habit she'd like me to lose."

Mitch chuckled. "Now that I think back on it, Hughes never has been real logical either." Damn. He had a revelation. "She never was just one of the guys, was she?"

"Hughes?" Grady sounded incredulous. "She's like any other woman. Strong, independent and opinionated."

"And don't forget compassionate, stubborn and sometimes unreasonable," Jackson added.

"By God, I wouldn't have Lily any other way." Grady stared into space, a wistful look in his eyes.

"Same here with Jordan. If I wanted a bromance, I'd have married you, McCabe." Jackson slapped him on the back.

"You both forgot the most important female adjective." Mitch narrowed his eyes at his beer. *"Unfaithful."*

Grady grunted. "Not Lily."

Jackson shrugged. "Hey, man, I get it. Your ex

screwed you over. But she's one woman. Doesn't mean you should paint every female with the same brush."

His jaw set, Mitch faced Jackson. "It wasn't just Luanne."

Jackson held his gaze, maybe waiting for Mitch to elaborate, but hell if he would air his dirty laundry to his buddies.

"Okay, so you've been screwed more than once. Same thing happened to Jordan. Her dad abandoned her and her mom when she was a baby. Then some jerk lured her here and ran off with all their money. She no more believed I'd hang around than one of the FBI's Most Wanted. What if she hadn't decided to take a chance and trust me?"

Mitch shook his head in disgust. "Don't talked to me about trust, Jackson." He stood, grabbing a twenty from his wallet and tossing it on the bar. "Yesterday I found Hughes kissing some other guy." As he stalked off, Jackson called after him.

From the corner of his eye, Mitch saw Grady catch Jackson and pull him back with a shake of his head.

On his way to the parking garage, Mitch stepped outside the double glass doors and saw a tall, dark-haired man headed his way. Mitch did a double take as he recognized Neil-the-SEAL.

Without stopping, he charged ahead and came nose to nose with the jerk. "What the hell were you doing at Alex's yesterday?"

The guy narrowed his eyes and his nostrils flared.

"What are you, stalking me? How'd you find out where I was staying?"

"I have my ways." *Yeah, it was called sheer luck.* "Now answer my question."

"My intentions where Alexandria is concerned are far more honorable than yours, that's for sure."

"Your intentions? What is this, Victorian England? How about we make this real simple." He planted his hands on the guy's chest and shoved. "Stay away from Alex."

Neil's face contorted in rage as he grabbed Mitch by his shirt collars and shoved him up against the wall. "You have everything I want and you don't even know it, you ignorant ass-wipe." He dropped Mitch and stared at his hands. Mitch couldn't believe they were trembling. So were his.

Neil looked Mitch in the eye. "I came to town to see if she'd give us one more chance, but she told me flat-out no. That she loved you." Neil sneered as his gaze traveled from Mitch's shoes to his eyes again. "What she sees in you is beyond me. But she's made her choice and I'm not it. All I have to say is you'd better treat her right or I'll come back and— Let's just say if you lose her, it'll be your own stupid fault." He turned and strode into the hotel before Mitch could form a reply.

ALEX COULDN'T BELIEVE her parents were really here. After her horrendous day yesterday, she'd never needed them more, and here they were.

She hated crying, but couldn't seem to stop tearing up. Especially when she caught Mitch ducking out of the ceremony. Alone.

"Here you go, sweetheart." Her mother handed her a wad of travel-size tissues from her voluminous purse.

"Thanks, Mom." It's a good thing she had the excuse of her promotion to use for her emotional state.

Dad came back from the refreshment table carrying two cups of punch and a plate of hors d'oeuvres, offering a drink to her mom.

Mom waved away the beverage and rummaged in her purse until she pulled out a camera. "Scoot closer to your dad, Alexandria." Alex stepped close and put her arm around her dad. He swiped off his ten-gallon hat and hugged her with both arms. Dad smelled like he always had, Old Spice mixed with leather and hay.

An avalanche of memories swamped her. Of working the ranch with Dad, following her brothers around, wanting to do everything they did. Hiding from her mom out in the barn. Dancing with her dad after the rodeos. Looking back on it now, her childhood seemed like a magical time.

Until Mitch's revelation the night before, she hadn't thought about how lucky she was.

"Say cheese," her mom called out and snapped a couple of pictures.

Grady and Lily and Jackson and Jordan approached and congratulated her. Alex introduced them to her parents, and her mom proceeded to take pictures of all of them together.

"Y'all want to come to dinner with us tonight to celebrate?" Alex invited the Gradys and the Jacksons.

"Thanks, Hughes, but we're going to stay in and take it easy tonight," Grady answered. The Jacksons also declined and were soon leaving the party.

"Well, baby girl, you gonna show us that new house of yours?"

Alex's heart tripped at the childhood nickname her dad had used when she was young. He hadn't called her that since her teen years when she'd obnoxiously told him not to. Now she was thrilled.

As nervous and excited as she was to show off her first home, Alex still felt the absence of Mitch. This would've been such a special day for them. She would love to have him meet her parents. But she refused to dwell right now. There'd be plenty of time for that later.

Her parents followed her in their rental car back to her home and she could see the pride and respect in her dad's eyes as he took in her tidy yard and freshly painted front porch.

Her mother, still snapping photos, walked through each room, scanning and nodding. Alex noticed how anxious she was for her mom's approval. Had always yearned for her mom's approval. Even as she'd been rebelling against everything her mother stood for.

"The front draperies are nice, sweetheart." Her mom finally spoke as Alex served them some iced tea.

"Maybe I could sew you some café curtains for the kitchen and bathroom windows?"

A warm glow filled Alex's chest. "I'd really like that, Mom."

"Al, get me the measurements on those windows, would you dear?" her mom called to her dad.

"Sure thing, doll."

As her dad found her yardstick and started taking measurements, Alex sat at the kitchen table with her mom and wrote down the numbers he called out. "Mom?"

"Yes, honey?" Her mother sipped her sweet tea.

"I'm sorry I never appreciated all you and Dad did for me." She covered her mom's hand and squeezed.

"Aww, honey. You just had to go your own way. And mamas don't like their babies going out into the big, bad world." Marge covered Alex's hand with her other one and squeezed back. "But you were always determined to see the world. And I'm proud of what you've accomplished." She shrugged. "So, you don't make pies and sew, but my goodness, honey." Her eyes widened. "You serve your country. And fly those big ol' jets!"

Alex laughed, stood and came around the table to hug her mom. "I love you."

"I love you, too, Alexandria."

"One of you want to stop the mushy stuff and write down these measurements?" her dad called from the hallway.

Alex grinned and grabbed the paper and pen and went to help her dad.

Mitch was right. She was lucky to have such a wonderful family, such a great childhood. Geez, she couldn't imagine what his must have been like. That little blond-haired boy, sitting there while his mom… Alex shuddered. How many times had he gone to bed hungry? She wanted to travel back in time and grab up that child and feed him and protect him.

But Mitch was a grown man now. And she couldn't do anything more for him.

"You all right, baby girl?" Her dad put his arm around her shoulder and brought her mind back to the present.

"I'm good, Dad." She smiled at her parents and they exchanged a look between them.

"We could tell you were upset before the ceremony. And you kept glancing at Major McCabe," her mom said.

"Didn't you write us about a good friend named Mc-Cabe? You two didn't even speak to each other today. Y'all have a falling-out?" her dad asked.

Alex tightened her jaw. She might as well tell them the truth. "I'm in love with him."

Her mom's eyes widened and her mouth dropped open. "Oh, honey."

"But it's just not going to work out."

"Oh, dear." Her mom stood and wrapped her in her arms. "I'm so sorry, sweetheart."

Her dad patted her tentatively on the back. "It'll be okay. What don't kill us makes us stronger, right?"

She tried to smile. "Right."

"Well, how about we go out to dinner at one of those fancy hotels on the strip and celebrate my daughter's promotion in style," he suggested.

Alex took them to the Venetian and nothing more was said about McCabe. The food was world-class, and afterward, she talked them into taking the gondola ride down the canal that ran inside the hotel.

As she waved them off at the airport the next morning, she promised to see them at Thanksgiving, and calculated that was only a little over a month away.

Wouldn't it have been the best Thanksgiving ever if she could've brought Mitch home with her? Maybe even been able to introduce him as her fiancé?

Hell, she'd have settled for boyfriend.

Who was she kidding? Right now, she'd give anything just to call him friend again.

17

Well, I'm not saving a $70 million plane, but...

Mitch had once heard of an unbelievable feat pulled off by a U.S. Navy pilot flying an F-35 joint strike force fighter.

This navy pilot had been lifting off from an aircraft carrier when his vertical thruster fired while he was still vectored for vertical takeoff. The plane headed nose-down, a hundred feet off the deck of the carrier. The aircraft should've crashed. Instead, the pilot performed a perfect vertical loop and then took off. Talk about stability control...

If Mitch hadn't seen video footage, he might have thought the whole story was merely urban legend. It seemed unbelievable that any fighter pilot would've had the kind of balls it would take to stay calm and get that F-35 to remain stable. So many things could've gone wrong. He was flying through his own afterburner. His wings had to remain perfectly level.

Sunday night Mitch lay in bed in his apartment, wide-awake, his hands clasped behind his head, and thought about that pilot. He came to the conclusion that if that guy could get himself out of that kind of snafu, then Mitch should be able to get himself out of the mess his life had become.

He'd left the MGM Grand shaken, Neil's words pounding in his brain. "You have everything I want and you don't even know it."

As if Mitch had been struck by a lightning bolt, everything he'd thought about his life had turned upside down at that moment, just like that F-35. And if he didn't want to crash and burn, he needed to execute a perfect vertical roll and get his life back in the air and flying right.

A part of him knew deep down that Alex had been telling the truth about her kiss with Neil. He hadn't really needed Neil's word to prove Alex's loyalty. But if he had acknowledged her truth the other night, that she loved him, he would have had to open his heart to trusting her. Like Jackson said, take a chance on someone.

Before he'd seen Alex kissing Neil, he'd been more happy, more—yeah, he needed to admit it—in love than he'd ever been with Luanne. But he might never have recognized it. He'd have gone through life—for as long as it lasted—thinking he could have Alex's love and still keep his heart safely inside the bunker he'd built around it.

Loving someone, trusting them, scared the hell out of him. It meant opening himself up to pain. He'd been there, done that and barely survived it. But the reason he'd survived it was...Alex. How blind had he been not to see she'd always been there for him? Twelve damn years she'd been there. Always standing beside him, watching his back, giving him her unconditional friendship. Her understanding. Her...love. She'd been his wingman, his buddy, his...everything.

He'd had the most wonderful gift all this time and never appreciated her. All these wasted years. Years of sleeping around, pretending he was the smart one, keeping women at a distance, using them for pleasure to get back at—what? His mom? Or a young girl who'd married too young to know what she wanted? What a jackass he'd been.

And Alex, wasting her time on a jerk like him.

Now it might be too late to get her back.

But he sure as hell intended to try.

Alex hadn't given up on him. He wasn't going to give up on her anytime soon.

THE WEEK AFTER her parents left seemed to pass by under a dark, heavy cloud of gloom for Alex. And, as if the weather wished to match her mood, it stayed dark and stormy all week, as well. Some nights it'd been too dangerous to fly, and Alex knew her students felt the same skin-crawling cabin fever she did at being cooped up in the classroom all night.

The weekend finally came and Jordan and Lily ambushed her Friday for a girls' night out. She knew they were trying to cheer her up, and she appreciated their effort, but...

Note to self: Jell-O shooters and broken hearts don't mix. Turns out she was a mean drunk. Ugh. She was totally embarrassing. Luckily, her two new friends had ignored her bad temper and self-pity party.

She spent the rest of the weekend in bed with the sniffles and actually called in sick Sunday night. By Wednesday she was forced to admit she needed a doctor and some antibiotics. The good thing about being sick was having an excuse for puffy eyes and a red nose. Someone else had to teach her class, but other than feeling guilty about that, being a contagious recluse suited her just fine.

She didn't seem to have the energy to care whether she ever left her house again. And she wasn't in the mood for visitors, either. This meant she might have left some well-meaning friends with the false belief that her house was full of infectious germs.

After another weekend in bed, even she couldn't stand herself. She'd milked the flu for all she could and it was time for her to cowboy up—as her grandfather would say—and face the world. A world without Mitch.

She shouldn't miss the clueless jerk.

But she did.

She missed being able to rant to him about her bad day. Or brag to him about her good day. She missed his smile, and his wicked humor. His optimism every day. Always finding some way to make life fun. She missed his kisses and his arms around her at night. Those exquisite moments of connection when he slid inside her and, for a little while at least, they seemed like one person. And she missed those moments of silence when she could look into his eyes and know that *he* knew exactly what she was thinking.

So, Monday night at the end of her shift, her mind had totally wandered off to thinking of all those things she missed about Mitch, wretched as that was. Leaning back in her chair, staring at the ceiling, she had her hands behind her head and her feet propped on her desk, completely oblivious to the emails and reports in front of her.

At the knock on her open door she dropped her feet to the floor and scooted her chair up to her desk.

Grady came in, looking almost as tired as Alex did. "Hughes, I'm heading out. You coming?"

"Doesn't Lily work days at her shop? Why do you look like death warmed up?"

He shrugged. "Just not a day sleeper."

"Blackout curtains help."

"Sounds crazy, but I just don't sleep as well if Lily's not there."

Alex tried to swallow past the huge lump in her throat. "No. It doesn't sound crazy."

Grady stared at her a second or two, and then gave her a brief nod. "Good night, Major Hughes."

"Good night, sir."

Over the past couple of weeks, she'd lain awake during the day, or been walking out to her car in the early morning hours, and wanted so badly to call Mitch. To see how he was doing, see if they could try to make it work just one more time, or just to hear his voice.

So far, she'd resisted. But in these dark hours just before dawn, when she was tired from working all night, her resistance was lowest. She yanked the paperwork toward her and tried to concentrate on performance reviews and grading classroom tests.

The later she worked the more quiet the building grew. She stuck in her ear buds and flipped on her iPod. Ugh! Why had she bought all these depressing songs about unrequited love? She flipped it off again and shoved to her feet. This was ridiculous. She could take this paperwork home and finish it there while she watched the DIY network.

Collecting her things, she grabbed her hat and headed out, locking her door behind her. Not that she had to worry about Mitch's practical jokes anymore— *Stop it, Alex!*

She had to stop thinking about him all the time.

Out in the parking lot she drew in a deep breath and

noticed the sun creeping up over the mountains, turning the sky pink and orange.

Feeling a bit better, she slid into her Mustang, dropping her briefcase in the passenger seat, stuck her keys in the ignition and turned.

The only sound she heard was a click. She knew better, but she still turned the key again. *Yep, same result, knucklehead.*

Man, she *so* did not need this right now. She was tired and cranky and hungry and all she wanted was breakfast and a bath. With a loud, self-pitying sigh, she climbed out, pulled the lever under the grill, and opened the hood.

She stared a moment, disbelieving her eyes. What the... How could a distributor cap just disappear?

"Looking for this?"

She jumped at the sound of Mitch's voice and peeked around the hood. He stood beside her driver's door holding a black distributor cap. Or more correctly, *her* distributor cap.

She blinked at him, uncomprehending at first. He'd removed her distributor cap? Why would he—

How could he—! He thought some stupid practical joke would make things right between them? Outwardly she bristled. But inside, her heart was melting at the sight of him. He looked like hell. He looked wonderful.

"What is this, McCabe?"

"Take it easy, Hughes." He stepped closer, but haltingly, like a cowboy gentling a wild pony. "I just wanted to talk." He gave her a sheepish grin and shrugged one shoulder. "Figured I'd make sure you couldn't get away."

She briefly closed her eyes and prayed for strength. Strength to resist running to him and wrapping her arms around him and begging him to kiss her. "All right." She folded her arms. "Talk."

He took another step closer and the breeze brought the scent of Mitch to her nose. She inhaled and felt a pang of desire burn through her.

"I remember the first time I saw you. We'd just entered the academy, and you were walking off the field alone after the swearing-in ceremony."

She frowned. "You saw me then?"

He nodded. "I remember thinking, hey, I'm not the only one that doesn't have family here. I'm not alone. So, I followed you."

"You did?"

"When I saw those creeps jump you, I wished to God I had a tire iron."

"You saw them?"

He nodded. "Didn't you ever wonder how I happened to be in that hallway?"

She shook her head. "I guess I was so shaken I didn't question it."

"You were shaken?"

"Scared to death."

"Well, you didn't show it. When I realized you'd taken down that upperclassman with your hands taped behind you, I couldn't believe it. And after, you were so tough, so determined to be treated equally." He ran a finger down her nose. "You never would let me protect you, or help you. I've always admired that."

Mitch's face swam before her. As if in a dream, the world slowed and brightened. A ray of sunshine escaped the shadow of the mountains and lit his blond hair in golden light. Her throat closed up.

He took another step and brought his fingers up to tuck back a strand of hair that had blown across her face. "Yet every time I lost faith in myself, you believed in me. You saw that better person in me even when I couldn't see it myself. I think I've probably loved you from the very beginning, Alex."

She tried to swallow, but she still couldn't speak.

"I love you, Alexandria Hughes."

She searched his eyes. Those baby-blue eyes that had smiled at her, laughed with her, beguiled her for twelve years. Then she looked at his mouth. Those masculine lips that had saved her, whispered both truth and lies to her. Lips that had hurt her and kissed her. "Say it again," she whispered.

He flashed a quick grin and then his expression turned serious again. "I love you, Alex. I love your stubborn streak and your horrible temper, and your sweet mouth and your deadly intelligence."

She punched his arm.

"Ow." He faked an expression of pain and rubbed his arm.

"It's about time, you idiot." She finally let the tears flow, even as she laughed.

Mitch smiled and gathered her into his arms and held her tight as if he never wanted to let her go. He caressed her back and laid his cheek atop her head.

She wrapped her arms around his waist and buried her nose in his chest. It felt so good to be in his arms again. To let herself be needy, after so many years of believing she couldn't show any sign of weakness.

He gathered her hair away from her wet face, and pressed kisses on the top of her head and her temple. "I'm so sorry I hurt you, baby." Bringing both hands up to cup her face, he lifted it to him. He bent and tenderly kissed her trembling lips. When he raised his head, he smiled at her. "Thank you for loving me all these years. For believing in me, even when I didn't believe in myself."

"It's always been you, Mitch. Always." She threw her arms around his neck and took his mouth with hers, luscious and long, happy and smiling, and never letting go.

Epilogue

HER MOTHER WAS weeping. Again.

"Mom, you're ruining your makeup." Alex grabbed a tissue from the dressing table and handed it to her mother.

"I know, honey, but I just can't help it. You're so beautiful."

Alex stood in front of the full-length mirror for a more realistic appraisal. She rubbed her scalp where the pins holding the small tiara and veil were digging mercilessly. The veil was attached to her hair so well, she could probably travel at the speed of sound right now and it wouldn't come off.

And the dress?

The ruched bodice had a halter neckline, which was okay, but the straps dug into the skin under her arms and the tulle under her full skirt was itchy. And don't even get her started about the freakin' long train. On someone else, it would be beautiful, she was sure. But she just knew she was going to trip and fall flat on her face.

She adjusted the waist one more time and scratched under her arm again.

"Will you stop twitching?" Jordan stepped close and smoothed down the skirt. "You look gorgeous."

"I just hate this." She stomped away and paced the distance to the end of the bridal ready room.

"Alex," Lily said. "Take a deep breath, close your eyes, and visualize—oh!" Her hand flew to her rounded belly. "She's kicking like a high-stepper in a marching band." She grabbed Jordan's hand and placed it on her protruding stomach. "Here. Feel that?"

Jordan's eyes widened. "Oh, Lily. It's a wonder you aren't black-and-blue."

Both of them turned to Alex. "Do you want to feel?" Lily asked.

"I, uh." Alex swallowed. "Nothing personal, y'all, but I think I'm going to throw up." She rubbed her chest where a cluster of nerves had taken up residence and were inviting the rest of the neighborhood for a party.

Her mom grabbed the bowl of mints off the coffee table, dumped them out and handed her the bowl. "Here, honey."

"Uh, thanks, Mom."

"Come here." Jordan led her to the sofa and sat down beside her. "What's wrong?"

Alex blinked back a stinging in her eyes. Her hands

were shaking. "Mitch has done this before and been hurt. What if he…changes his mind?"

"Oh, honey." Her mom came to sit in a club chair kitty-corner to the sofa and patted her hand.

"What if he decides he doesn't want to take a chance on us? What if—"

"Alex, I'll tell you what," Jordan said. "When you start to walk down the aisle, and you first see Mitch, you look in his eyes. And if you still doubt his love for you, you just turn around and run out of the chapel and I will personally explain to Mitch and everyone, okay?"

Alex stared into Jordan's confident face. Jordan had been there, done that. She'd walked down that aisle and seen the look in Jackson's eyes. Alex remembered that look. Had been downright envious of it at the time. If Mitch looked at her that way…

She nodded. "It's a deal." Then she smiled. This was her freakin' wedding day!

There was a harsh knock on the door and Lily went to answer it.

Jackson peeked his head around the door frame. "Uh, ladies, Major McCabe would like a Sit Rep?"

"Tell him we're ready to begin," Alex called to him as she stood and smoothed down the elegant skirt of her stunning wedding gown. She was ready. After twelve years. It still seemed a bit surreal. But she'd wanted Mitch for so long now, to know they would finally be together. That he wanted her. Loved her. He'd even requested reassignment to a desk job so they could be married and she could still fly with her squadron.

He'd always supported her ambitions, her right to be treated equally. That's why she'd gone behind his back and requested the desk job for herself. She loved flying, but she'd been there, done that. She didn't have anything else to prove. And besides, she also loved the idea of having a kid or two with Mitch.

She couldn't wait to tell him tonight. In bed.

Jordan gathered up the record-long train, and Lily took Alex's mother's hand. They exited the bridal room, made it down the hall and turned the corner, and then it was all really happening.

Alex could hear the string quartet playing the wedding march when the door opened for her mother to go through, then Lily, then Jordan. And then it was her turn.

She stepped through the door and saw her father in an elegant black tux waiting with his elbow extended, and slipped her arm through his. He was blinking a lot and his jaw was tight, but he held his shoulders back and his chin up.

As she made her way down the aisle, she saw all three of her brothers standing in the front two rows with their wives and kids, and behind them sat aunts and uncles and cousins. The rest of the pews on both sides of the aisle were taken up with friends and colleagues.

Lieutenant Colonel Ethan Grady, her squadron

commander, her friend and mentor, stood as grooms-
man, tall and rock-steady in his uniform. He'd been a
steadfast presence in her life ever since she'd come to
Nellis. A man of integrity and resolution.

She remembered last year when she'd been so worried about Lily hurting him. Lily had seemed so flaky,
and yet somehow she'd managed to soften his tough
exterior and bring a spark of warmth to his cold and
lonely existence. It was hard to believe at almost forty
years old, Grady was going to be a father for the first
time.

Next to Grady stood Jackson. Wickedly handsome
in a black tux, he still had eyes only for Jordan. When
Alex met Jackson he'd been the consummate adrenaline junkie, risking his life for his country and for the
thrill. She remembered being terrified after hearing
he'd been shot down. He'd barely survived.

And the night Mitch had made that horrible bet with
him. Alex had been furious. But Jackson had met Jordan that night, and now look at them. The former thrill-
seeker now found excitement and adventure in being a
cop and loving Jordan.

Alex's attention moved from Jackson, the best man,
to…Mitch.

She looked into his eyes.

Mitch stared back at her, his gaze so intense, so filled
with love and awe and confidence that the power of his
emotions washed over her and flooded her with a love
so strong it made her chest squeeze tight. It filled her

so completely there was no room for thought, no room for doubt.

Feeling a ton of weight lift, she smiled and walked the last few steps toward her soon-to-be husband. Her daddy kissed her cheek and handed her arm to Mitch, who took it while still staring into her eyes. The force of his love hit her again as she felt his warm hand close around hers and they turned together to the reverend.

The reverend started to speak and that's when panic hit her hard.

She froze and bit her lip. "Um, Mitch?" she whispered out the side of her mouth.

"Yeah?" He glanced at her, his eyes darkening with worry.

"My mind's a complete blank. I've totally forgotten my vows." Her voice was quavering.

He looked at her and flashed that gorgeous grin, his dimples twinkling. He squeezed her hand. "No worries, Hughes. I've got your back."

* * * * *

COMING NEXT MONTH

Available September 27, 2011

You can find more information on upcoming
Harlequin® titles, free excerpts and more at
www.HarlequinInsideRomance.com.

HBCNM0911

REQUEST YOUR FREE BOOKS!
2 FREE NOVELS PLUS 2 FREE GIFTS!

red-hot reads!

*Harlequin Romantic Suspense presents the latest book
in the scorching new* KELLEY LEGACY *miniseries
from best-loved veteran series author Carla Cassidy*

*Scandal is the name of the game as the Kelley family fights
to preserve their legacy, their hearts...and their lives.*

Read on for an excerpt from the fourth title
RANCHER UNDER COVER

*Available October 2011
from Harlequin Romantic Suspense*

"**W**ould you like a drink?" Caitlin asked as she walked
to the minibar in the corner of the room. She felt as if she
needed to chug a beer or two for courage.

"No, thanks. I'm not much of a drinking man," he
replied.

She raised an eyebrow and looked at him curiously as she
poured herself a glass of wine. "A ranch hand who doesn't
enjoy a drink? I think maybe that's a first."

He smiled easily. "There was a six-month period in my
life when I drank too much. I pulled myself out of the bottom of a bottle a little over seven years ago and I've never
looked back."

"That's admirable, to know you have a problem and then
fix it."

Those broad shoulders of his moved up and down in
an easy shrug. "I don't know how admirable it was, all I
knew at the time was that I had a choice to make between
living and dying and I decided living was definitely more
appealing."

She wanted to ask him what had happened preceding
that six-month period that had plunged him into the bottom

of the bottle, but she didn't want to know too much about him. Personal information might produce a false sense of intimacy that she didn't need, didn't want in her life.

"Please, sit down," she said, and gestured him to the table. She had never felt so on edge, so awkward in her life.

"After you," he replied.

She was aware of his gaze intensely focused on her as she rounded the table and sat in the chair, and she wanted to tell him to stop looking at her as if she were a delectable dessert he intended to savor later.

Watch Caitlin and Rhett's sensual saga unfold amidst the shocking, ripped-from-the-headlines drama of the Kelley Legacy miniseries in

RANCHER UNDER COVER

Available October 2011 only from Harlequin Romantic Suspense, wherever books are sold.